GROWING VINES

Plate 1. The author's vineyard in late summer, at Cranmore, I.O.W.

GROWING VINES

N. POULTER

Amateur Winemaker

Published by

Amateur Winemaker

Argus Books Limited
1 Golden Square,
London W1R 3AB,
England.

1st IMPRESSION 1972
2nd IMPRESSION 1976
3rd IMPRESSION 1977
4th IMPRESSION 1978
5th IMPRESSION 1980
6th IMPRESSION 1981
7th IMPRESSION 1983
8th IMPRESSION 1984
Reprinted 1987

ISBN 0 900841 67 2

Printed in Great Britain by
The Garden City Press Ltd., Pixmore Avenue, Letchworth, Herts. SG6 1JS

DEDICATION

To Robert and Margaret Gore-Browne, whose vineyard first inspired me and from whom I have received so much help in the field of viticulture.

CONTENTS

ILLUSTRATIONS

6

Figure	*Page*

Introduction

The British have been so indoctrinated with the fallacy that they do not have the climate for outdoor grapegrowing that it is hard to persuade them otherwise by argument alone. Gradually, however, the man in the street is coming to believe in the revival of winegrowing in England and Wales, and quite often he will at least have heard of one of the new commercial vineyards or perhaps know an amateur who has a few vines in his garden.

This book is intended primarily as an aid to these amateurs and it is hoped that those readers who do not already grow their own outdoor grapes will be encouraged to join the thousands who do. Grapegrowing, for both winemaking and dessert use, is one of the most rewarding and satisfying pastimes there is and it must be regretted that there is so little written on the subject in English. With isolated exceptions, most of southern England and Wales is suitable for unprotected garden grapes and indeed early varieties will flourish a long way north in good site. In all but the cooler areas there is no need to have a sunny wall or similar protection; the English commercial vineyards are after all in open fields.

All that the grower has to do is plant suitable varieties and follow certain simple rules. Grapes that are not properly ripe will never produce good wine, no matter how much sugaring is done, and some varieties will never ripen here. This should come as no surprise; the Germans, for instance, obviously do not plant the same varieties as the Spanish. There are several vine varieties which are well suited to *our* own conditions and their culture, as I shall explain, is well within anyone's capabilities.

I hope that the reader will find discussed here every branch of the subject that will affect him or her as a small grower. I have tried to present the facts simply and those aspects and practices unsuited to our climate or to the amateur are not mentioned. I am now a partner in an English commercial vineyard but started grapegrowing as an amateur with a few vines in my garden in the

Thames Valley. As a result of my early difficulties in obtaining guidance on the subject I have tried to put into this book all that I would have liked to have known when I started myself.

There is a world of difference between growing a small plot of vines for family wine and investing £40,000 in a commercial vineyard and winery, and those who like myself wish to grow commercially will have to acquire greater knowledge than it is the intention of this book to give you. A bibliography appears in the Appendix for those who want to go deeper into the subject.

The main aim of this book is to encourage the culture of outdoor vines, but I include a chapter for the increasing number of gardeners whose interest also lies in the greenhouse.

N. Poulter

CHAPTER 1

The History of Vinegrowing in England

Much of the early disbelief in the possibility of an English viticultural revival stemmed from some rather quaint ideas of the history of grapegrowing in this country. It is not commonly understood that the former decline of winegrowing in England was the result of not one but several factors.

Much of it is shrouded in the mists of time, but there is a surprising wealth of records of viticulture, and enough to show us what happened. Very briefly the story is as follows. . . .

We know from the vessels found in his graves, that British Iron Age man drank wine, but at this early date it is most likely that all the wine drunk in Britain had in fact been grown further south, and was imported here in the course of trade. By the time the Romans had occupied the country the vine had made its appearance, and it seems that it is they who introduced the plant. It was one of the many gifts Britannia received from Rome. When the Romans eventually left these shores, their successors continued to culture the vine, and in the Saxon period many references were made in the manuscripts of such as Bede and in the laws and accounts of the kings and landowners. One chronicler of the time said of the Isle of Ely that "it is so thickly planted with apples and vines that it is an earthly paradise", and in fact the area became known as the Isle of Vines.

The first comprehensive list of vineyards appeared after the Norman conquest, in the Domesday Book. This great work of 1088 detailed some thirty-eight vineyards in England, giving their size and sometimes their output. These vineyards were often extensive, one at Belcamp in Essex owned by Ralph Baignard, for example, being eighteen arpents or about twenty-three acres in extent. The future of English viticulture at this period seemed assured and then in 1152 Henry II married Eleanor of Acquitane and the first blow fell. Part of Eleanor's dowry was the Garonne district of France and with it the prolific wine producing area near Bordeaux. Suddenly it was possible to import large quantities of cheap wine. It is likely that the quality of English wine was little if at all inferior, but it was much more expensive to grow. The English land-owners reasoned that it was better to import cheap southern wine and put their own vineyards to a more profitable use. Land suitable for arable use was scarce, and wheat and barley were always in need. The vineyards did not completely disappear overnight but they began to dwindle. Some were ploughed up and fewer were planted.

Then, in the middle of the fourteenth century, there was a small but significant climatic change and the summers became less favourable. Some vineyards still continued but their profitability was less certain. By the sixteenth century most of the remaining vineyards were in the hands of the ecclesiastical orders and with the dissolution of the monasteries by Henry VII between 1536 and 1539, vineyards as a regular feature of the countryside ceased to exist.

From that time on viticultural ventures were infrequent and isolated. Vineyards such as that owned by Colonel Blount in the time of Charles II at Blackheath appeared from time to time but they were no longer common. Towards the end of the eighteenth century a vineyard of some repute was planted by Charles Hamilton at Painshill in Surrey. The vines were of two varieties; the Auvernat, a grape from Burgundy, and the Loire, and the Pinot Meunier of the Champagne. At first vintage red wine was made but it proved to be harsh. After that only white was made. The grapes were picked as late as the season allowed and care was taken to prevent premature fermentation taking place by transporting the grapes from the vineyard in small containers, thus avoiding self-pressing. Fermentation was carried out in hogsheads and judging by contemporary accounts it was usually fairly violent. Obviously quality was taken seriously as only the juice from the first two pressings was used.

After fermentation the wine was racked off into clean hogsheads, and in March a fining was carried out by means of the application of fish glue. Soon afterwards the wine was bottled and it was said to be fit to drink as soon as six weeks later. It was not a long-keeping wine and it was best drunk before it was more than a year old, denoting that sulphuring was probably not done. The quality was generally agreed to be excellent and the selling price of 7/6 to 10/6 per bottle at that time speaks for itself. At one sale alone 500 poundsworth was sold to a single London wine merchant at a rate of fifty guineas a hogshead. But it seems that even in an age of eccentrics Charles Hamilton was considered eccentric and when he died his vineyard seems to have died with him. Either he left no heirs or they were incompetent vintners.

A hundred years later the last of the historic winegrowing ventures was started by another eccentric, the Marquis of Bute. In 1875 he planted five acres of vines at Castell Coch, north of Cardiff. After a few trials he decided on the Gamay Noir. Several poor years in a row as the vines were coming into bearing did not help and success did not come easily. However the Marquis was both wealthy and determined, and another five acres were planted in 1886 at Swanbridge in the Vale of Glamorgan. A temporary planting was also made at St Quentins' near Lowbridge. But it seems that neither wealth nor determination made for true success and in the forty years of the vineyard's existence only seven vintages were reported to be good. In 1916 the vineyards were ploughed up to produce food for the war effort and they were never replanted.

Had a more suitable variety been selected, success might well have been achieved. It had obviously become accepted at this stage that the vine was unable to flourish this far north and it was plainly heretical to question this dogma. Those few who tried to grow vines usually grew totally unsuited varieties and used incorrect pruning methods, and their failures merely reinforced the fallacy that the vine was a tender and difficult plant, with no place in England.

Fortunately during the first half of the twentieth century much had happened in the viticultural world. Many new varieties had been produced in continental research stations, and a lot had been discovered about the metabolism of the vine and what the plant required in the way of conditions and treatment. In the 1950s a few pioneers realised this and some considered it worth while trying once again to re-establish the vine in England. Many trials had to be carried out and much had to be learned by experience. It was found, for example, that a variety did not always behave in the way it might have been expected to. Some very promising varieties failed while others which had seemed less promising thrived, but it soon became evident that certain varieties in certain localities would not only ripen their fruit but could produce excellent wine. The old myth was shattered at last.

In 1966 there were only seven acres of commercial vineyards in the whole of England. Since that time planting has increased at an accelerating pace, and the area must now be in the region of 1,000 acres. The bulk of this acreage has been planted in the last few years and so it is not all bearing yet. Even when it does, the total annual crop will amount to only two or three million bottles – a mere drop in the ocean. These vineyards are generally between four and ten acres in extent, although some are larger. Just how much more the industry will continue to expand depends on several factors and it is impossible to predict its eventual size. Nevertheless it seems likely that the English wine industry will become a significant part of the agricultural scene. Unfortunately it has so far been a Cinderella industry and has had to haul itself up by its own boot straps, because Officialdom is only just beginning to show lethargic signs of a shift from its initial indifference. This is none too soon when one considers that those first 1,000 acres alone will contribute about £3,500,000 annually to the exchequer in duty and VAT.

A line from an old Burgundian song still sung at the wine sales festivities held at Beaune runs: "May the English never have the vine, the pretty vine". But now the English have it, and with care they intend to keep it.

14

CHAPTER 2

The English Climate

It has already been implied that we tend to have a national inferiority complex about our climate, but how many have really taken the trouble to compare it to that of the northerly continental winegrowing regions? The answer is very few, for those who have done so will have realised that much of our country compares very favourably. We often hear such comments as "It rains all summer here", and yet the fact is that most of the country suffers an agricultural drought more than five summers in every ten. Others say "We don't get enough sun", and yet a few areas in England get more than almost the entire German winegrowing region and many more receive equal amounts. As for frosts, we have less dangerous late spring frosts than they do on the continent and our less severe winter frosts present no dangers at all.

The vine is not the tender difficult plant some would have us believe. It is tough, very hardy in winter and amazingly adaptable. The most important climatic factors as far as the vine is concerned are those of rainfall, sunshine hours and air temperature. Taking rainfall first, there is no part of the country too dry for mature vines although young vines in dry spells require watering just as any other plants do. A very few places which are generally confined to high places do have excessive rainfall, but as they are usually mountainous or moorland they are inclined to be too elevated and cool anyway. Our June/July period which is the flowering period is usually drier than the same period on the Mosel and this helps our vines to set good crops of fruit.

As for sunshine hours, different varieties require different amounts, and most of the varieties which thrive in this country are affected less by direct sunlight than by temperature. Those who think that vines require sunlight all through the day are mistaken. It may be an advantage, but it is not as important as people often believe. Many varieties do well when they get direct sunlight for a maximum of only three hours in any day so if you have a garden which loses the sun for much of the day do not be discouraged. Table 1 shows how well we compare with the continent for sunshine.

When it comes to temperature, there is a difference between the season we expect here and that normally experienced in Germany. This difference is not.so much in the *amount* of heat we receive as in the timing. For example, in the hottest months of July and August the average temperature on the Mosel may be one degree higher than the temperature, shall we say, on the Thames, but in September and October, the very important ripening months, the average temperature on the Thames is often *more* than one degree higher than that on the Mosel. This tendency is due to our oceanic climate with its more temperature but longer growing season. Gardens, in fact, have some advantages over the larger commercial vineyards, for while the garden is usually sheltered by houses, trees and fences the large vineyard is exposed to the wind. As a result the air temperature in the average garden will often rise far above that experienced in a large vineyard.

Table 1 makes comparisons between sites in this country and some in northern continental winegrowing regions. It can be seen that we compare not unfavourably.

Table 1 – Comparison of English and continental climatic data (30 year average).

Locality	Rainfall total April–Oct. (mm)	Sunshine hours April–Oct.	Heat total April–Oct. (degree-days over 8°C)
ENGLAND			
Cambridge	319	1182	1142
Cheltenham	399	1142	1163
Kew	359	1147	1262
Norwich	399	1229	1129
Plymouth	484	1272	1129
Sandown	388	1385	1326
Tunbridge Wells	408	1268	1102
GERMANY			
Ahrweiler (Ahr)	401	1061	1204
Bernkastel (Mosel)	443	1193	1326
Trier (Mosel)	443	1259	1378
FRANCE			
Rheims (Champagne)	369	1312	1369

FROST PRECAUTIONS

The vine is no more susceptible to frost damage than the apple, except that the apple usually bears its blossom higher off the ground. The only time of the year when the vine is likely to suffer frost injury is in spring when the buds have burst. As this is not usually until May, frost damage is not common in all but bad frost hollows. If dwarf apple trees are often damaged by frost in your area, you may have difficulty with your vines, but covering the canes with newspaper when frosty nights are forecast will usually provide a simple and effective protection.

CHAPTER 3

Vine Varieties

The choice of the correct variety of vine is of the greatest importance. Many people think of the vine as if it were just one variety and believe that they all require the same climate. This is very far from the truth, for some varieties will thrive where others will fail miserably. The variety Black Hamburg, for example, is grown in the open vineyard in Alsace, but in England is suited only to the cold-house. Yet how often we hear of someone wasting their time growing Black Hamburg out-of-doors here!

There are probably as many as thirty varieties which will grow well and ripen their crops in England, but some are so much better than others that it is not worth cultivating more than a few. New vine varieties are produced only by crossing two other varieties, and the chance of producing a new vine which is even as good as its parents is about one in ten thousand. It can be seen therefore that vine breeding is not an easy task and growing vines from pips is generally a complete waste of time.

The European vine, although existing as many different varieties, is really only one species, (*Vitis vinifera sativa*). In the USA this did not exist before it was introduced there by man, but there are several other species which are native to the USA such as *Vitis Riparia*, *Vitis Labrusca*, *Vitis Berlandieri*, etc. The American species produce juice which is greatly inferior to that of the European vine. They do tend to be more vigorous, however, and for this reason and in the effort to produce more disease resistant varieties, attempts were made to cross the European and American vines to produce offspring with European quality and American heavy cropping.

In viticulture the term "hybrid" is applied only to those varieties which owe some of their ancestry to one of the American species. The first hybrids a hundred years ago, produced not only American vine vigour but also the comparatively poor juice quality. More recently however, hybrids have been produced which not only produce prolific crops but also have good quality juice of European character. Many of the varieties we grow in Europe are crosses between pure bred European varieties such as Siegerrebe whose parents are Madeleine Angevine and Gewurztraminer. The offspring of pure European parents are called "crosses", *not* hybrids. There are in addition one or two very good hybrids grown, for example Seyve Villard 5276, which is very popular with amateurs due to its heavy crops.

White grapes can, of course, only produce white wine, but red grapes can produce red, white or rosé depending on whether the grapes are pressed straight away or put into the fermenting vats for a certain time. In northerly latitude some of the red varieties actually produce a better white or pink wine than they do red. All the finest wine in northern regions is white, though this is not to say that good red wine cannot be grown. English red wine is like that of Germany, being fresh and fruity, but it is not likely to be truly great. Those readers who have drunk German red wine will know that it is more like a heavy rosé, but they will also know that it *can* be delightful.

People often ask what variety they should grow to produce a sweet or a dry wine. The answer to this one is that any variety can make either a sweet or a dry wine depending on what the vintner wants. Commercially speaking, with the exception of some special wines such as Auslese, all wines are fermented dry and then sweetened to suit the market.

As so often happens in nature, fruit growing near the limits of its climatic range is unequalled in quality and English grapes are no exception. English wine can be of an unsurpassed excellence.

The varieties listed below are not the only varieties which will grow here but they include the best available to the amateur. Some excellent varieties have been produced by some of the continental breeding stations but unfortunately they are seldom available for amateur planting.

The ripening period of grapes varies according to variety, site and weather. Outdoor vines will ripen their crop between mid-September and early November, though most are ready to pick in mid-October. One cannot lay down hard and fast rules but in descriptions given here it may be taken that "early" means ripening before the end of September in most years. Midseason grapes ripen during the first three weeks of October, and "late" varieties after that. Of course dates vary a little from year to year, but very wide differences from the norm are rare.

OUTDOOR WHITE VARIETIES

Mueller-Thurgau (roughly pronounced Moo-le-Tour-gow) (Plate 2). This variety is popularly known as Riesling Sylvaner but it is now believed to be a Riesling x Riesling cross. It is widely grown in Germany, accounting for about 20% of all vines planted. It is also widely grown in England on a commercial scale, producing a wine which is frequently superior to that produced from the same grape in Germany. It is a well proven grape of really excellent quality. The bouquet is wonderfully flowery.

Seyve Villard 5276 (Seyval blanc) (Plate 3). A very popular vine in England with the amateur due to its heavy crops. This means that those with only room for one or two vines can still produce a reasonable quantity. The juice from this vine on its own tends to make a wine of neutral character and it is a good idea to blend in a proportion of Mueller-Thurgau juice. **An ideal mixture for those who wish to produce both quantity and quality is one Seyve Villard to one Mueller-Thurgau.**

Madeleine Angevine (roughly pronounced Mad-el-ane Onj-veen) (Plate 3). A heavy cropper of very good flavour for both eating and winemaking. This is a very early variety and therefore especially suitable for those living in a cool area. It is a highly reliable cropper even in the most unfavourable years.

Madeleine Sylvaner. Probably the earliest of all varieties to ripen in this country. Another fine dual purpose grape ideal for less favoured sites.

20

Plate 2.   Mueller-Thurgau – early October.

Plate 3.   Seyve Villard 5276 – September.

Chardonnay. A comparatively late season ripener which seems to do best in inland areas. It is really only suited to winemaking, yielding a product with a good Chablis character.

Pinot Blanc (Plate 4). Similar in general appearance to Chardonnay, but in my opinion a superior variety. Late season, but even in the awful summer of 1980 it gave us a fine wine in considerable quantity. Not widely planted in England at the time of writing, but I am sure it soon will be.

Traminer. Famous for its spicy, full-bodied Alsatian wines. It needs the benefit of a warm wall to ripen well in this country.

22

Plate 4.   Pinot Blanc – mid October.

23

BLACK OUTDOOR VARIETIES

Wrotham Pinot (roughly pronounced Rootam Pee-no). A very interesting variety which is the descendant of vines grown in ancient English vineyards. It is really an early strain of Pinot Meunier which is grown in the Champagne. Not surprisingly it is well suited for the production of sparkling wine and is probably the best vine for this purpose in England.

Seibel 13053 (Plate 5) (roughly pronounced Sigh-bell). Undoubtedly the best grapes for the production of red wine in this country. Cropping is very heavy, ripening is early or mid-season and the wine is fruity with a good colour. This variety used to have a dubious reputation due to some fallacious rumours. After faulty experimentation carried out many years ago it was believed that the substance Malvidin 3.5 diglucoside found in certain grapes, including Seibel, was responsible for liver damage, (in chickens). This work has since been totally discredited and you may safely drink the wine from Seibel grapes without any worry of toxicity.

Pirovano 14. Well suited to the cooler parts of the country due to its early ripening. It is a grape that also makes a good eater owing to its large berries and good flavour.

Baco 1 (Plate 6). A very vigorous grower needing plenty of room. It should be planted only on a house or garage or shed. It is also attractive on a pergola providing shade in the summer. Red wine from this grape tends to be a little harsh but a very nice pale pink wine can be made by fermenting only the juice.

Brant. Another vigorous variety requiring almost as much room as Baco. The wine is ordinary, Seibel making a better red wine, but one of the great attractions of this vine is its magnificent autumn leaf colour.

24

Plate 5.　Seibel 13053 – early October.

Plate 6.   Baco – mid October.

CHAPTER 4

The Site, Soil, and Spacing

The commercial grower this far north will if possible find a
southerly slope, though some use level ground and at least one
large vineyard in Kent is planted on slopes which are mainly
northerly in aspect. This is not the disadvantage it might at first
seem because of the good shelter offered from the prevailing,
cooling southwest winds during the summer.

As mentioned before, the amateur in his garden will often have a
more favourable microclimate than that found in the open
vineyards, so do not think it is necessary to have a veritable
suntrap. Those who have fences and walls in their garden will find it
convenient to use them for vines, but vines on trellises in the open
are more usual and of course this is the only way in which they will
be found in large vineyards. If you do use walls, although a south
facing wall is best, there is nothing to stop your using a wall which
faces east or west. Experience has shown that vines which get direct
sunlight for no more than three hours in a day still flourish in most
areas.

The soil is naturally important to any plant but the vine is
tolerant of a very wide range of types. Reasonable drainage is
desirable but the vine will thrive in the heaviest clay as long as
surface water can run off in the winter.

If the soil is sandy or particularly light it is of course important to
fertilise it more often than other soils as the nutrients will be
leached out more easily. Do not believe the old wives tale "the
poorer the soil, the better the wine", although it might be truer to
say that the vine will flourish in soil that will grow little else.

While clays may sometimes present drainage problems and can be cold and heavy to work, they are usually very fertile. If your soil is sodden for most of the year, including the summer, it must be drained. In particularly difficult sites where proper drainage is not possible vines may be planted in substantial mounds or ridges which provide a good volume of free draining soil. Our vineyard is very heavy clay, being extremely sticky in the winter and like concrete in summer if not tilled, but our vines flourish and bear lovely crops. Liming heavy clay will improve the soil structure considerably.

If you have a *very* chalky soil and your vines make slow growth, you can do much to modify the soil around the vines by digging in humus and manure, (not mushroom compost, which is usually lime-laden), and by using acid-reaction fertilisers. In very difficult cases vines that have been grafted on to 41B rootstock should be grown.

A vine is after all like any other plant and if not fed it will produce poorer crops each year and may eventually stop bearing altogether. Even when a soil is fairly well supplied with nutrients, the vine will remove some of these each season with the crop, leaves and canes, and what is removed must be replaced one way or another. Farmyard manure or compost is very valuable, not so much for the food it contains, which is very little, but mainly because it helps to keep the soil biologically active. Plants need carbon dioxide during the day in order that they may carry out photosynthesis, and the soil bacteria supply much of this by breaking down organic matter.

In addition to organic matter the vine needs mineral salts which are most conveniently added in the form of fertiliser compounds. No soil is exactly the same as any other but, assuming that your soil is in reasonable balance, the table on p. 30 will give you a fertiliser programme that should suit your vines. In addition, if the soil is deficient in lime it is a good idea to turn in chalk at a rate of 120 gm per sq metre (4 g/sq yd) every two or three years. The ideal soil pH is around 6.5.

Your vines are really the best indicator of how well balanced your soil is. Meagre growth and pale leaves are usually a sign of nitrogen deficiency. If the vine takes on a really yellow appearance in the summer it is probably suffering from chlorosis which is due to an excess of lime or a deficiency of magnesium in the soil, causing an imbalance, which renders it difficult for the plant to take up iron. The application of magnesium to the soil in the form of Epsom salts or the use of related iron fertilisers such as Sequestrine should solve the problem. Incidentally, it is always preferable to *correct* a soil imbalance rather than bypass it if possible.

The appearance of leaves which become yellow in the areas between the main veins is a sign of magnesium deficiency, whereas older leaves showing a bluish discolouration of the upper surface indicate a lack of phosphorus. Leaves browning and dying from the edges sometimes mean that the plant is short of potassium.

There are several other elements that the vine requires for health but most of them are required in small quantities and few soils are badly lacking in these trace elements. If you suspect or have it confirmed that your soil is deficient in these substances there are several compound fertilisers readily available to the gardener which will rectify the situation.

The fertiliser programme overleaf is for mature vines. Young vines in their first two years of life need only half the quantity of fertilisers recommended. Specially compounded vine fertilisers are obtainable from some suppliers (see Appendix).

Within reason herbaceous plants may be grown right up to vines as long as they do not shade or crowd them. In this way it is possible to grow vines at the back of normal flower borders.

It is most important that any *summer* application of nitrogen is not added until after the flower has set its fruit or it will cause poor fruit set. Summer nitrogen is only necessary if growth is weak. Over-vigorous growth is nothing but trouble.

SOIL CULTIVATION

To prevent compaction of the surface due to walking around the vines and to control weeds simple cultivation should be carried out from time to time. Fertilisers should also be hoed in. Do not dig too deeply around vines for some of the roots run within a few inches of the surface. These day-roots are of great importance in taking up nutrients and although they will grow again if damaged, their temporary loss can be harmful at certain times of the year.

Table 2 – Fertiliser programme for mature grapevines.

Time of application	Fertiliser	Application rates. Quantities expressed in grammes per square metre (oz/sq yd in brackets)
March/April	Nitrogen	Dried blook 90 (3) or Ammonium sulphate 75 (2½)
	Phosphorus	Bone meal 75 (2½) or Superphosphate 45 (1½)
	Potassium	Potassium sulphate 75 (2½) or Muriate of potash 45 (1½)
	Compost or manure	2–4 kg per sq metre (4–8 lb/sq yd)
July (*After* flowering) Only necessary in case of weak growth	Nitrogen	Ammonium sulphate 60 (2)

VINE SPACING

With the exception of very vigorous varieties such as Baco and Brant, which need about three metres (10 ft) between them, all varieties mentioned in this book should be spaced at approximately 1.2 m (4 ft) intervals. If two or more rows are planted along side each other, the rows should not be closer than 1.2 m, and commercial vineyards usually have their rows separated by 1.5–1.8 m (5–6 ft) to allow the passage of machinery. Rows planted too closely make working between them difficult and risk encouraging mildews through lack of ventilation.

Theoretically the rows should run north and south so that both sides of the trellis receives an equal amount of sunshine, but in my experience this is quite unimportant.

Plate 7.   Vine rows in late June.

CHAPTER 5

Planting, Training and Pruning

As far as growth is concerned vines may be conveniently divided into two groups, one having "normal vigour" and the other "high vigour". All varieties mentioned in this book with the exception of Baco and Brant are of normal vigour. Training for each type is a little different and so they will be dealt with separately here. The following applies to the normal vigour vine and differences in the treatment of the others will be covered later.

1st YEAR

Late March or early April. Planting is normally carried out in the spring although it can be done at any time during the dormant period from the end of November to late April. Some nurseries are able to chill-retard plants for planting up until mid-June. The soil should be prepared by fertilising and digging over well, before the vines arrive. When the plants do arrive they need not be planted immediately if there is no time, but they should in any case be unpacked and have their roots lightly heeled in under moist but not sodden soil. They may be left like this for a few days without coming to any harm from frost or drying out. There is generally no advantage in planting a vine of two or three years of age. A one year old vine will fruit just as quickly because an older vine still has to establish a new root system. Further, a one year old vine may be trained exactly as you wish from the beginning.

As can be seen from Plate 8 the plant is very simple at this stage having roots at one end and a small shoot at the other. If you receive a plant with more than one shoot, remove all but the strongest with a sharp pair of secateurs. If the roots are longer than 10 cm (4 in), cut them back to this length, and similarly cut the one shoot back to two or three buds. When planting dig a hole about 30 cm (12 in) deep and 30 cm in diameter. Mix a little *well rotted* compost with the top soil portion and ensure that it goes back around the roots, which should be spread out well. The depth at which the roots should be depends on the soil. If it is very heavy the roots should be about 10 cm (4 in) deep, but if it is light they should be a little deeper. Do not have them so deep that the shoot is closer than 5 cm (2 in) to the soil surface.

The plant should be firmly heeled in as this helps the root development. Unless the soil is very wet, the vine should be watered. A good 1.5–1.8 m (5–6 ft) bamboo should be firmly pushed into the soil as close to the vine as possible.

May. In this month the buds will swell and burst unless the plant is particularly slow in getting away. When the first of the tiny new shoots is about 2 cm (¾ in) long, select the most robust and rub out all others. During this first year you must allow *only one* shoot to grow, the idea being to concentrate the strength of the plant into this new stem. As this new green shoot is so close to the ground in the first year it runs the risk of damage by a late spring frost if there is one. Therefore it is a good idea during this month to keep an eye on the weather forecast, and should there be a frost warning you can cover your young vines with weighted newspapers. This will effectively protect the plants from being nipped and set back a while. The shoot should be loosely but firmly tied to the bamboo every 15 cm (6 in) or so to prevent it being damaged by the wind. As the leaves grow it will be noticed that a little bud will appear in the axil of each leaf. This is illustrated in Plate 13.

These buds will break into small lateral shoots and these should be rubbed out at an early stage to prevent them sapping strength from the main stem. A second bud will appear later next to the first but these should be left untouched as they will develop into the following year's shoots and they will remain dormant this year.

June to August. The single stem continues to grow and laterals are constantly removed as they appear. This removal of laterals is only done in the first and second year of the life of the vine.

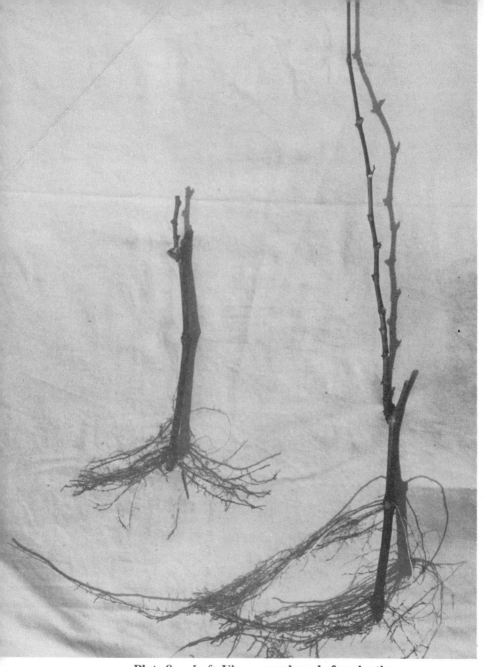

Plate 8.   *Left:* **Vine pruned ready for planting.**
Right: **Vine as lifted from nursery.**

Plate 9.   Vine planting – roots spread out.

Plate 10.   Vine after planting.

Plate 11.   Vine, one-year-old, before pruning.

Plate 12.   Vine, one-year-old, after pruning.
(cut back to 2 or 3 buds)

Plate 13. Growing shoot showing leaf axils with lateral shoots and dormant bud at top of picture (next year's fruit bud).

39

September. From this month onwards laterals should be allowed to grow on. Towards the end of this month the growing top few inches of the main stem are pinched out to assist the stem that has grown to ripen. The length of the stem will depend on the variety, the soil fertility and the type of weather that has been experienced during the summer. It may be as little as six inches or it may be more than sixteen feet. Normally one may expect three or four feet of growth. If it is less do not worry because some vines take a little time to find their feet, but at the same time check that you fed the vine, with fertiliser, especially if you have a light soil.

October to December. The vine may now be left alone. The leaves will fall in October and November and by the end of the year you will have nothing but a bare cane.

2nd YEAR

January and February. The course of action you take now depends on how much wood your vines produced in their first summer. If the cane grew vigorously and you have more than three or four feet of ripe healthy wood as thick as a pencil, then you should proceed as for third year treatment, and you may have a small crop of grapes in the coming summer only eighteen months after you planted the vine. It is more normal, however, to find that the first year cane is either rather short or spindly. First of all you must find out how much of the cane is ripe wood because the top will usually have died back a little. Taking a pair of sharp secateurs and working from the top, cut back bud by bud until you reach living dormant wood. This is easily recognised by its pale green inside and brown outside. The outer colour will vary from straw to deep red-brown depending on the variety. When you have reached this point you know that what you have left is healthy wood and at this stage you decide whether you should proceed as for third year treatment or not. It has just been said that the remaining cane is often rather short or spindly, and if this is the case you take your courage in one hand and your secateurs in the other and cut the cane back to only two or three buds. You may wonder what you have achieved in a season. The answer is not only 10 cm (4 in) of new cane; it is that the vine has now established its roots and in the

Plate 14.   Two-year-old vine being pruned.

Plate 15.   Tying down cane for first time at end of second year.

coming summer it will produce a shoot of much greater vigour which will bear the first crop in the following year. Plate 12 illustrates the first winter pruning of a typical vine.

April. The buds on the pruned back cane swell.

May to September. The buds burst in May and you should carry out exactly the same procedure as you did in the first year. One shoot only is allowed to grow and all laterals are removed until September. At the end of September the growing tip is pinched out as before.

October to December. The leaves will fall, leaving a bare cane which will, as mentioned before, be much stronger and longer than it was in the first year. The dormant buds along its length will produce the fruiting shoots in the coming year.

3rd YEAR

The principles of pruning are very simple, the two most important facts being firstly that the fruiting shoots always grow from canes grown in the previous year, and secondly it follows that by governing the amount of last year's cane you leave on the vine, so you govern the size of the potential crop. Never be tempted to overcrop your vines; after all, it is no use producing an enormous crop if it doesn't ripen, for loading unripe grape juice with sugar will still make bad wine. The size of the crop you get will depend on several factors such as the year's weather, the vine variety, the vine age and the soil fertility. The first crop your vines bear will be only about half the weight they will bear two years later. Vines taking up only four feet of wire may give as little as two or as much as fifteen pounds of grapes, whereas vigorous vines such as Baco or Brant may give as much as fifty pounds of fruit, although of course a much larger space is needed to bear it. The highest quality wine is produced from normal vigour vines.

January and February. You should now inspect your vines and prune each back bud by bud as before, then any cane which is left longer than 1.5 m (5 ft) should be cut back to that length. If you have a little less than 1.5 m (5 ft) do not worry.

At this time you should set up your wire trellis. If your vines are planted by a wall or fence make sure that the wires are at least 10 cm (4 in) from the wall or fence otherwise the fruit will be liable to damage by wind later. If the vines are planted in the open, the wires should be stretched between posts set firmly in the ground and anchored with stays if the rows are to be very long.

Plate 14 shows the arrangement of wires. One cane supporting wire (2.5 mm) is stretched at a height of 60 cm (24 in) above the ground. Over this cane wire are stretched pairs of wires (2 mm), each pair having 5–8 cm (2–3 in), or the thickness of the supporting posts, between them. The first pair is stretched about 24 cm (9 in) above the cane wire and further pairs are stretched at 30 cm (12 in) intervals up to 1.5 or 1.8 m (5 or 6 ft) above the ground.

Now taking each vine in turn count ten buds from the point where the cane grows up past the cane wire and cut off the remainder (Plate 15). What is left is bent on to the cane wire, twisted a few times around it and secured at the tip just inside the last bud with a tight tie. If the wire is well tensioned this method makes for a very rigid system which will not move and chafe in the wind. Some care is needed when making the bend which should be fairly tight so that the cane is held firmly in position. A tight bend will also restrict sap flow enough to encourage strong shoots at the top of the vertical part of the cane, (the stock), which can be used as replacement canes described below.

Bends should be made in the middle of an internode, that is the section of cane between two buds. Bends attempted at nodes will almost certainly result in breakages. Plate 18 illustrates cane bending which must be done gently but firmly. Grip the cane tightly with both hands almost touching, easing with the thumbs. The cane will frequently creak, but this does no harm. Success comes with practice and it would be a good plan to get this by bending any surplus wood already cut from the vine to get the feel of it. Occasionally a cane will snap no matter how careful one is, but if it only splits half way through it is still useable and should bear as well as one that is undamaged. If the cane is very thick or the internodes are very short it is a good idea to make the total bend over the distance of two internodes, being careful not to put pressure on the node in the middle.

Never be tempted to bend down too much too soon as this will

**Plate 16.   Vine at end of third year after bearing first crop
– before pruning.**

Plate 17. Vine at end of third year after pruning, before bending down.

46

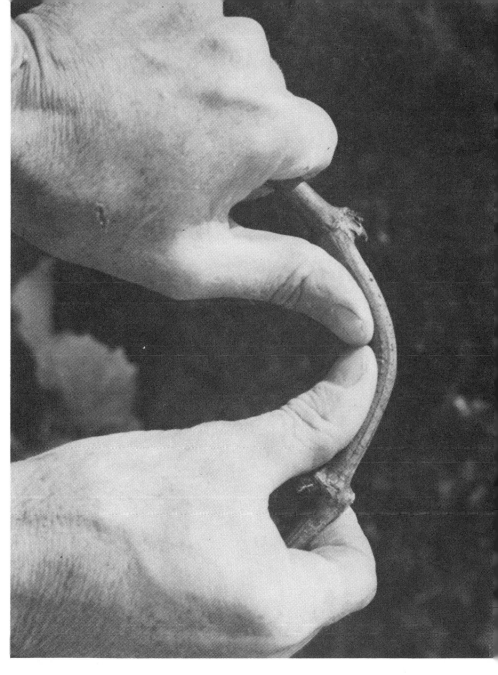

Plate 18.   Bending vine cane.

Plate 19.   Vine at end of third year after pruning and bending down.

result in weak growth which provides nothing in the way of replacement canes which will be required next year. If in doubt as to the cane's suitability for bending down it is much wiser to cut it off level with the bottom wire and let just the topmost three or four buds break.

April. The buds along the cane swell.

May. The buds burst and the fruiting shoots commence growth. Any shoots which appear from the vine within 15 inches of the ground should be rubbed out. The bottom 15 inches or so of the vine will become the permanent stock or trunk of the plant. No further disbudding should be done as you have already fixed the number of fruiting shoots by your pruning. The buds which burst along and just below the cane-wires should be allowed to grow unchecked as fruiting shoots. Removal of shoot laterals is now neither necessary nor advisable.

June. As the fruiting shoots grow they should be tucked in between the pairs of wires. This keeps the growth neat and allows the maximum penetration of light to the leaves. The pairs of wires may be loosely clipped together if necessary now and then.

Often it is necessary to tie in growth, particularly when the trellis has only single wires. The best and cheapest material to use for this is wire-reinforced paper strip. This is obtainable precut into lengths, five inch being the most suitable. These are at present marketed as "Twist-Ems" or "Fasties" and are stocked by most garden shops. Pass the tie around the shoot and wire, allowing *plenty* of space for growing expansion. Cross the ends of the tie at right angles and twist together three or four times. . . This instruction might seem a little basic, but I have so often seen shoots cut by too tight a tie, and others break free because the twisting has not been thorough.

During the month or even during the previous month the flower buds will appear and gradually become more prominent. The time blossoming actually begins will depend on the variety and the weather, but it is usually in late June or early July. *Under no circumstances* should outdoor vines have their fruiting shoots pinched out a few leaves above the flower as is often suggested in old books. Far from helping the flower to set its fruit is more likely to throw the flower and give a poor set. The fruiting shoots should be allowed to grow on until they pass the top pair of wires which will not normally be until late July or August. The leaves are the factories of the vine and the further north the grower is, the more leaves he needs on his vines to produce the sugar for the fruit. As the flower appears early in Summer the crop will always be born low on the vine.

July. If flowering did not take place in June it will do so in this month. All the varieties mentioned in this book are self pollinating, but one hopes for dry weather during the flowering period to assist pollination although a little rain does very little harm. The fruit sets quickly and the tiny young grapes appear and slowly swell.

We sometimes tend to forget that fruit is not produced for our benefit, but for that of the species. Whether we think of apples, acorns or grapes, they are produced only for propagation. It is pure chance that some fruits are palatable purely as an aid to seed dispersal, but we have been able to improve their palatability and fruitfulness by means of breeding and selection over the centuries. But how do fruits arise? Not always as one might think – simply between blossoming and harvest. Most perennials, including vines, take around 15 months to produce a crop.

If we look at our vines in late summer we see only this year's grapes ripening, but next year's have already been initiated and lie hidden as embryo flowers within dormant buds. In the axil of each leaf – that is the angle between the leaf stalk and the stem – there are two buds. One breaks soon after forming, to become a lateral shoot. The other remains dormant until the following season. The word "dormant" really only describes the outward appearance. Inside the cells are busy dividing and differentiating into various organs so that the bud soon becomes a highly compressed and packaged shoot complete with leaves and flowers.

This differentiation takes place during the latter half of July and throughout August, in fact the six week period immediately following the flowering of the current year's blooms. It might justly be said that the vine at this time bears two crops – one as visible grapes, the other invisible as next season's potential crop, which

Plate 20. Pinot Blanc – flower bud, early July.

Plate 21.   Pinot Blanc. *Left:* **Flower in bloom.**
Right: **Flower just set – mid July**

will lie dormant during the coming winter and emerge as next summer's flowers. The number of potential flower clusters within the bud is variable and depends to a great extent on the weather during the differentiation period. If it is warm, many embryo flowers will be formed, but if it is cold, the number will be few. Therefore it will be appreciated that a large crop is not just the result of a good summer in the year it is picked, but also of a good summer the previous year. This was illustrated by the exceptional summers of 1975 and 1976, yielding larger than average crops in 1976 and 1977. Fortunately we do not need exceptional summers to give good fruit bud differentiation. The summer of 1979 was by no means special, but the amount of flower born in 1980 was excellent even though its promise was denied because of rotten weather during flowering. This indicates the second condition for a good crop. The weather for pollination and fertilisation must be adequate when the vines finally flower. In this country, this is in late June or more usually in the first half of July.

THE FLOWERS

Vine flowers are born in clusters, between one and three generally being born on each fruiting shoot. The flowers are an insignificant pale green, and before opening the clusters resemble tiny bunches of grapes. The method by which the flowers open is unusual. The petals do not part from the apex like those of a buttercup, but split from the flower stalk end towards the apex so that the five petals, still joined, are shed as a little cap or calyptra. The stamens bearing the male, pollen-producing anthers then straighten and elongate. They are arranged around the female ovary consisting of two compartments each containing two ovules, which, once fertilised, become the pips or seeds. Surmounting the ovary is a short style terminating in a stigma which exudes a syrup designed to trap pollen grains and encourage them to "germinate". At the base of the ovary, alternating with the stamens are nectaries, but in spite of these and a light but attractive flower scent, pollination is hardly ever aided by insects.

POLLINATION

The optimum requirement for pollination is a warm, dry spell. At such times the anther pollen sacks are more readily dessicated and ruptured to shed their grains. With the assistance of air currents these grains become trapped in the sticky stigmatic fluid and pollination is complete. Fertilisation has yet to take place. It entails the growth of a pollen tube down through the style to an ovule. At least four pollen grains are required to fertilise the four ovules and achieve total success. The more ovules fertilised, the larger will be the grape, all other things being equal. In fact it is common for hundreds of grains to arrive at each stigma, and all compete in the process. Fertilisation is achieved as soon as the grain nuclei unite with those of the ovules, and fruitset may be said to have taken place. Sometimes a heavy downpour of rain or an unseasonal cold snap during flowering will upset fruitset and result in bunches containing infertile berries. These will fail to develop and either fall off or remain tiny and hard.

Nearly all vine varieties have self-fertile flowers and do not need pollinators, but a few, particularly some originating in America, have imperfect flowers. This means that they have inadequately developed male or female reproductive organs. If you have a vine of unknown variety and it consistently fails to set fruit it is possible, though uncommon in Britain, that it is one with imperfect flowers. Careful inspection of the flowers with a magnifying glass might enable you to determine this. Flowers lacking properly-formed female organs (staminate) exhibit very small or non-existent ovaries. Those with imperfect male organs (pistillate) have stamens which, instead of standing around the ovary like a crown, are recurved downwards away from the pistil. In either case self-fertilisation will be poor or impossible.

From all this we can see that a grape crop has two important hurdles to overcome and the critical time is from late June to the end of August. During this period this year's are formed. If conditions are right for these processes, varieties suitable for our climate will ripen their fruit regardless of the weather during the remainder of the season.

August. Those fruiting shoots that have grown through the top pair of wires should be trimmed off a few inches above the top wire.

Plate 22.   Vine rows in late August.

Plate 23.   Harvesting time at Cranmore.

Plate 24. Pruning secateurs and (below) grape cutting shears.

Ordinary hedge shears will do the job perfectly well. Lateral shoots that stick out untidily may also be trimmed back and mature vines at this time of the year take on the appearance of neat hedges. The fruit will continue to swell and start to ripen towards the end of the month. Ripening begins when white grapes take on a translucency and black grapes begin to colour.

September. Ripening becomes more marked and early varieties such as Madeleine Angevine and Siegerrebe may become fully ripe in some areas before the end of the month. Bird nets should be put up at the beginning of the month.

October. Ripening continues to completion and the harvest usually takes place around the middle of the month or maybe the end of the month in cooler areas. The date you decide upon for your vintage will depend on the variety and the weather. A few extra warm sunny days in the autumn will quickly add a little more sugar to the juice in your grapes, so if the summer has been poorer than average and the autumn is fine, take advantage of it. Only experience can really teach you when you should harvest, and short of pressing a few bunches and using a hydrometer, which is wasteful, or using a refractometer, which is expensive, you will have to rely on your judgment. In southern England or Wales all those varieties mentioned in this book should be ripe by the end of October at the latest unless you happen to live in a particularly cool spot.

As far as tasting for ripeness is concerned *beware*! Different varieties have different levels of juice acidity at the same sugar content. For example Mueller-Thurgau juice is low in acidity compared with Seyve Villard and if you taste a Mueller-Thurgau grape of say 18% sugar and then a Seyve Villard grape of 18%, the latter will not taste as sweet even though the sugar content is the same. Experience alone with the varieties you grow will enable you to estimate the approximate degree of ripeness by tasting.

Always try to harvest your grapes in dry weather. Not only is it much more comfortable but rain will reduce the gravity of the juice and dilute the flavour. Grape bunches can carry a lot of water between the berries and obviously this is undesirable in the must.

If you use secateurs for the harvest *take care*! It is so easy after picking for a while, to become careless and take a finger tip off. If you can obtain them, get hold of a pair of grape cutting shears. These can still give you a nip but they will do no serious damage. On no account pick grapes that you cannot process the same day. Once grapes have been taken from the vine they will begin to deteriorate due to wild yeast ferments and juice oxidation. A brief description of the vinification will be found in Chapter 10.

November and December. Leaf fall takes place and the vine is left to ripen its wood.

4th YEAR

January and February. You have now reached the stage when you will carry out winter pruning as it should be carried out year after year. If pruning were not carried out the vine would grow larger every year but it would bear a crop that would never ripen. Winter pruning is designed to keep the vine both in shape and from growing larger and larger. The vine will now appear rather like that shown in Plate 25.

Plate 25.   Vine at end of fourth year before pruning.

Plate 26. Vine at end of fourth year being pruned.

Plate 27. Vine at end of fourth year after pruning, before bending down.

Plate 28.   Vine at end of fourth year after pruning and bending down.

What you must do now is to replace the old cane you bent on to the cane-bearing wires last year with new cane. Ideally, instead of replacing it with one long cane it is better to replace it with two short canes bent down on to the cane-bearing wires in opposite directions. This system of pruning is called "Double Guyot", (pronounced Gee-oh with a hard G). In Plate 26 canes (a) and (b) have been selected as replacement canes, and cane (c) has been selected for providing a short two or three bud spur. Replacement canes are chosen for their quality as well as their position. They should be neither too thin nor too thick, the ideal diameter for most varieties being 7–10 mm (¼–¾ in). If they are very spindly they will probably have poor fruit potential, and if too heavy will bend badly. The optimum internode length is about 10 cm (4 in), but this is not so important. Cuts are made as shown and the old unwanted wood is removed from the wires leaving the vine as in Plate 27.

Two canes are each cut back 10 buds and they are bent down on to the cane-bearing wires as shown in Plate 28, their ends being firmly tied to the lower wire. Do not worry if they overlap the neighbouring vines. Experience over the years will tell you the optimum number of buds to tie down in order to balance the growth potential of the vine. Too few buds will result in excess vigour and unruly growth; too many buds will result in weak shoots and possibly too great a crop to ripen properly. Each bud is after all going to produce a fruit-bearing shoot. If your vines are reasonably robust try tying down a total of 20 buds and adjust in future if required.

The short spur is left mainly to increase the chances of good replacement canes growing near the stock, although the shoots it produces will usually carry fruit too. Spurs are selected if possible from canes which spring from the old wood of the stock and their main object is to keep the vine in shape, for it will be readily understood that if you constantly take replacement canes from the previous year's *main* canes these replacements will spring further and further from the stock each year. Therefore we utilise the periodical appearance of watersprouts or shoots from the old stock, to reshape the vine as required.

Every year from now on you should carry out Double Guyot pruning as described above. The best time of the year for this operation is in January or February. At this time the vine is properly dormant. If the vine is pruned too late in spring it will "bleed" sap. This is not really serious although it used to be thought so, nevertheless it is best avoided if possible. Also canes which are not bent down on to the cane-wires before bud burst will throw most of their growth at the cane extremities.

TRAINING "HIGH VIGOUR" VINES

Vigorous varieties such as Baco and Brant need much more room than others. As a result it is convenient to train them and prune them differently, the main difference being that instead of having a small permanent stock they have a large permanent framework on which there are several spurs.

During the first two years of the life of these vines training is little different from the procedure described for "normal vigour" vines. If a sturdy cane is grown in the first year it is cut back only to the height at which you wish the fruit to be carried. If you are growing these vines on a house, this height will be determined by such features as windows and doors. If growth is weak in the first year cut the vine back to a few buds and in the second year allow only one bud to develop so that the desired height will then be achieved as in Fig. 1.

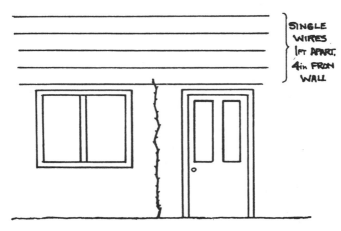

Fig. 1.   High vigour vine cane at desired height.

In the following summer the top five or six buds are allowed to grow as fruiting shoots, all other buds lower down being rubbed out as in Fig. 2.

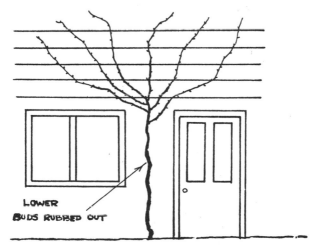

Fig. 2.   Top six shoots after leaf fall.

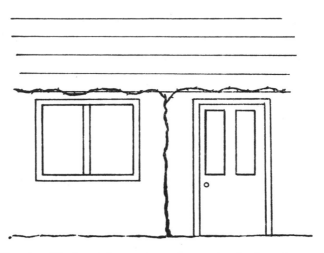

Fig. 3.   Horizontal arms bent down – beginning of season.

At the end of the year the two sturdiest canes are selected and bent horizontally in opposite directions. You will have to use your judgment as to their length. They should start at around six feet each though in later years they may be extended up to 10 feet.

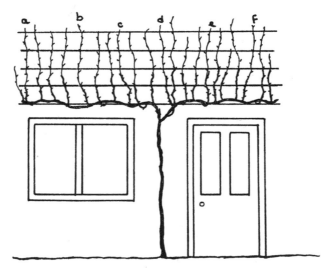

Fig. 4.   End of season.

64

These arms will form a permanent part of the vine frame but for the first year of their life every bud along their length will become a fruiting shoot so that by the end of the season the vine will appear something like Fig. 4.

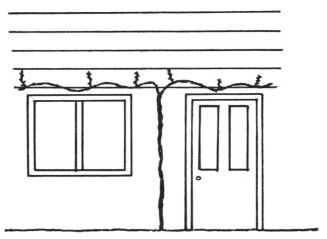

Fig. 5.   Vine pruned to spurs – beginning of season.

Fig. 6.   Spurs at end of season.

So far training has been only slight variation of the "normal vigour" vine procedure, but from now on instead of replacing each arm of the vine every winter a number of spurs is left along each arm. In Fig. 4 canes a b c d e f have been selected to be cut back to four or five bud spurs while the remaining canes are completely removed. The distance between spurs should be about two feet and after pruning the vine will look like Fig. 5. In the following spring all the buds on the spurs will develop into fruiting shoots as in Fig. 6, and in the next winter and every winter after that the strongest cane from each spur is cut back to four or five buds as a replacement while all the others are removed as in Fig. 7. From time to time watersprout canes can be used to provide new spurs and keep the vine in shape.

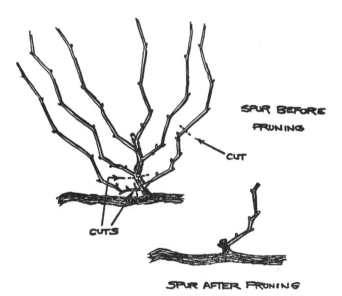

SPUR BEFORE PRUNING

CUT

CUTS

SPUR AFTER PRUNING

Fig. 7.

CHAPTER 6

Vine Pests and Maladies

The vine, like all plants, is susceptible to certain ailments and pests although there is no reason why any of them should cause the grower serious concern as long as sensible precautions are taken. All the hazards likely to be met in England are discussed below and the means of combating them is given.

Mildews. There are several mildews which attack the vine from time to time but fortunately they may be easily and cheaply prevented by a sensible spraying programme. Anyone who suffers serious damage to his vines due to bad mildew only has himself to blame. There are three forms of mildew which are more common than any others and happily the treatment we use to prevent them also effectively prevents the others.

Downy mildew or Peronospora (*Plasmopara viticola*) effects both the leaves, which turn brown and die, and the fruit which shrivel and become leathery in appearance. The German name for this disease in Lederbeeren which means literally "leather berry", and grapes infected with this fungus will not ripen. The old form of treatment was Bordeaux mixture and it is still used in some parts of Europe, but one of its disadvantages is that every application retards vine growth for up to three days and obviously if several applications are made throughout the season, the vine growth may be retarded for a fortnight. Modern treatments employ materials such as Mancozeb, Zineb or, more readily available to the amateur, Murphy's Liquid Copper Fungicide. Downy mildew is not very common in Britain because it is encouraged by warm, wet conditions. Our climate is usually cool and wet or warm and dry.

However it is most unwise to ignore the possibility of an outbreak because so much damage can be done if one's vines are infected. There is also the likelihood of a similar mildew, Rote Brenner, (*Pseudopeziza tracheiphila*) which favours the cool wet weather we frequently experience in the spring. The most obvious symptoms are brown leaf patches which turn quite red before whithering. Fortunately the fungicides mentioned will deal with both diseases.

Fig. 8.   Grapes infected with peronospera

A mildew requiring a different fungicide is Oidium or Powdery Mildew (Uncinula necator) (Fig. 9). This disease affects all parts of the plant. The first sign on grapes is a white dusty appearance followed by splitting and blackening of the berries. No further ripening will take place. Sulphur effectively prevents Oidium but it is wiser to use a wettable form as opposed to Flowers of Sulphur which if applied too heavily can cause leaf burn. Baco is sulphur-shy and should not be sprayed with sulphur but it is resistant to Oidium anyway.

Wettable sulphur is not easy to come by in small quantities, but Murphy's Systemic Fungicide is effective and easily obtainable.

Fig. 9. Grapes infected with oidium.

This compound will also prevent Botrytis or Grey mould. Most people are familiar with it on such fruit as strawberries. By keeping other mildews in check and by keeping the vines healthy by feeding them correctly, the risk of Botrytis infection is much reduced as this fungus cannot penetrate the skin of the grape unless it is first damaged by some other agent. The most common symptoms of Botrytis are the bunch stems turning brown and drying up, causing premature bunch drop, and the berries turning pinkish grey and growing fuzzy coats of mould. Botrytis is undesirable on red grapes at any time as it destroys the red pigment in the skin, but white grapes destined for winemaking do not suffer badly as long as they are infected when they are reasonably ripe. In fact most readers will know that certain wines such as the French Sauternes and the German Auslesen actually depend on this fungus infecting their grapes to produce their beautiful flavour. So long as your grapes are moist inside when you pick them do not discard them, revoltingly rotten though they may look! If on the other hand part of the bunch is quite dry it should be cut out or it will impart a musty taste to the wine.

Though infected berries may be used, the juice yield will be diminished and for this reason if for no other it is sensible to take every precaution to prevent infection. The disease can spread very rapidly and lead to complete crop spoilation. Dessert grapes will of course be ruined by attack at any stage. Botrytis spores are ever present in the air. They can attack any damaged vine tissue under almost any conditions, though moist weather, particularly if accompanied by wide differences between day and night temperatures, is most dangerous.

Fig. 10.   Grapes infected with botrytis.

Dead-arm (Phomopsis viticola) was once thought to be of minor importance, but it now appears to be more of a menace than was once supposed. Vines in a weakened state due to a waterlogged soil or nutrient deficiency, are most vulnerable, but when climatic conditions suit the disease it can appear anywhere. Ripened canes in the winter show a silvering of the bark and are peppered with tiny black specks, (not to be confused with the larger lumpy black spots of botrytis sclerotes, (over-wintering bodies). If the infection is light no other symptoms may appear, but often buds fail to break in the spring and whole canes may die back. Liquid copper used during the summer will help harden the plant tissue and prevent attack. Winter wash with a product such as Ovamort or Mortegg will also help, but I must confess to being in two minds about winter washes. They undoubtedly clean the dormant wood of pests and diseases, but they also kill hibernating predators such as ladybirds which often infest the vine bark. In our vineyard we have come down against winter wash, but I do not think one can be pedantic about it.

A very unpleasant, but fortunately uncommon mildew is Penicillium. I have only seen it twice in the past eighteen years, and then only locally, but grapes showing signs of it must be discarded. If used for winemaking very strong off-flavours can appear. The mould usually appears associated with botrytis, but unlike the grey fuzz of botrytis, penicillium is sky-blue.

Mildew prevention by Spraying

Mildew must be prevented rather than cured, for once it has got a hold it is usually impossible to do more than control further spread of the disease. Failure to carry out a sensible spraying programme is very likely to lose you your crop, and vines which are infected badly year after year may soon be destroyed.

In 1971 a great many growers in Spain must have bitterly regretted not having sprayed, because that summer mildew reduced the Spanish wine output to a trickle. Being very dry there normally they do not expect mildew trouble and do not spray very often, but in that year they paid the price. In our far more humid conditions it is simply asking for trouble not to spray preventitively. Peronospera and botrytis must be guarded against all season, and although Oidium is only supposed to be dangerous in hot weather, with our variable climate it is sensible to spray for this disease just as often.

Vines are open to attck from the moment of budburst until the end of the season, and it is wise to be prepared for the worst and assume that all the mildews are just waiting for a chance to take advantage of the lazy grower. If you do get mildew in your vines it nearly always *is* due to laziness because the simplified spray programme given in Table 3 is really very little trouble.

Table 3 – Fungicidal spray programme for the prevention of mildew

Malady	Conditions most favouring development	Fungicide
Downy Mildew	Warm and wet	Murphy's Liquid
Rote Brenner	Cool and wet	Copper
Botrytis	Any damp weather	
Dead arm	Cool and wet	Murphy's Systemic
Powdery Mildew	Warm and dry	

Apply both fungicides together at the rate recommended by the manufacturer at 10 to 20 day intervals from late April (budburst), to early October (not less than two weeks before harvest). For obvious reasons the wetter the weather the more frequent the spraying should be. Ideally this should be carried out on a dry day with dry weather forecast, but do not keep putting off spraying in a prolonged damp spell. If the fungicides are on the vines for no more than twelve hours before being washed off by more rain they will at least take care of spores then emerging, and some spray will stick on under the leaves for a longer period.

In the past it was unwise to spray during flowering because the earlier chemicals used could upset the blossom. *It is still unwise to apply copper during flowering*, but the systemic compound is safe if applied at the proper rate with a fine mist nozzle, and fortunately the two mildews it combats, Oidium and Botrytis, are those which are most dangerous at this stage.

Insects and related pests
Phylloxera. We, in England, have a tremendous advantage over the continental grower in that one of the worst pests of all is not endemic here. This pest is *Phylloxera vestatrix*, a little aphid with a very complicated life cycle and a disastrous effect on the European vine on the continent. The only effective method of fighting this pest is to plant only grafted vines which have resistant rootstocks, as the most dangerous attack is to the roots. In England the extra cost of grafted vines is rather a waste of money as the chances of

Phylloxera ever establishing itself here are remote. The climate is generally unsuitable and the vineyards too widely spaced to encourage spread.

More important, it is the policy of our Ministry of Agriculture to keep our shores free of this pest by means of the compulsory destruction of any infected plants.

In the dozen appearances that have occurred in England in the past one hundred years all have been stamped out at source. Destruction would also apply to grafted vines because although they can tolerate the pest, they can also harbour it. I am in total agreement with this policy on the grounds that it is sheer stupidity to admit any pest into Britain if we can avoid it. Apart from the dangers of the insect itself it almost certainly acts as a vector for virus diseases. Ministry policy renders the use of grafted vines in this country an irrelevance. Indeed grafted vines suffer several disadvantages.

Ungrafted plants are highly adaptable regarding soil types and will live and bear well for centuries, whereas grafted vines need carefully selected rootstocks to suit different soils, and they need to be uprooted and replaced after about twenty years. They are also subject to graft failure problems, suffer more under conditions of stress and are more expensive. Our vineyard is about half grafted and half ungrafted, the latter performing better consistently.

Red Spider. Occasional and isolated attacks by this mite may be experienced but they are easily treated by spraying with any suitable insecticide obtainable from your garden shop. It is wise to spray insecticides only when and where you have to, because of course both harmful and beneficial insects are destroyed. The usual symptoms of Red Spider attack are malformed growing shoots and lace-like brown-edged holes in the leaves. Mild attack is unimportant.

Wasps. In the average year wasps are of little concern as the grapes ripen after the wasps have started to decline in numbers. However if you have an early variety or the summer and autumn has been particularly favourable for wasps, these insects can be very troublesome. The only really effective treatment is to find the offending nests and destroy them but this is seldom possible. The old fashioned trick of putting down jars of water and jam or beer and vinegar can be most effective, but it will not stop attack of the grapes completely. Do not be tempted to put polythene bags over the grapes for although you may keep the wasps off you will almost certainly get bad mildew instead!

Rabbits. If you live in the country where rabbits abound you will doubtless be fully aware of the damage they can do to plants. Mature vines are not quite so likely to be attacked but young vines are very attractive to these animals, and one inch wire netting should either be put around each vine or around the area.

Deer. Many parts of the country have a surprisingly high population of wild deer, and where present they present a formidable problem. If deer have access to your land the only answer is a wire net fence eight feet high!

Birds. In the large open commercial vineyards in England birds can be an enormous problem. In the garden, however, it is a simple matter to net your vine area and be protected completely. As it is not necessary to put up the nets until the beginning of September and they are taken down when you pick around the middle of October, the nets will last for years if handled carefully. If you decide on a particularly large planting or if netting is for some reason impracticable you will have to resort to a number of deterrents. Most deterrents are effective for a while but birds will get used to anything, so scaring devices such as bangers, coloured balloons, and tinsel must be changed every other day. The most troublesome birds are Blackbirds, Songthrushes and Mistlethrushes, and the most vulnerable grapes are the black varieties.

Failure to produce Flower. Vines grown from pips are hardly ever worth the effort, one of their faults sometimes being that they are sterile, (and in any case never come true to variety), but known varieties also on occasions produce no flowers. This can be a temporary fault due to unusually bad weather during the flower bud differentiation period of the previous summer. Excessive foliar vigour due to soil over-rich in nitrogen may also discourage flower production. This effect can be aggravated by a deficiency of potash or phosphorus.

Failure to set fruit. Plants sometimes bear abundant flower which then fails to set. This may be due to withering of the blossom by botrytis, or cold, wet weather causing "coulure". In this case the pollen is either washed from the flower by heavy rain or the temperature is too low to allow the pollen nuclei to migrate to the ovules. Lastly the vine may be one with imperfect flowers, which are either incapable of being fertilised or require a pollinator variety nearby.

WEED CONTROL

Any plants growing amongst vines offer competition for the available nutrients, water, light and air. A little light weed cover is of no significance except that it prevents the soil warming up and so has an effect on the air temperature, but some weeds propagate rapidly and others become very large quite quickly, and it is wise to prevent any growth at all if possible. If you have time you can hand weed and hoe, but many of us have a hundred-and-one other things to do without spending hours weeding. Fortunately there are now several excellent herbicides which if used sensibly keep your vines free of weeds safely.

Before mentioning the right herbicides to use I should point out those which should be avoided at all times. Obviously one should never use compounds such as Sodium chlorate because this will permeate through the soil and kill everything whose roots it contacts. The so-called "hormone" type weedkillers such as 2,4,D or worse 2,4-5,T should never be used anywhere near vines which are even susceptible to fumes which might be given off for several days from a treated area many yards away. Fumes from a neighbour's lawn which has been treated with a selective herbicide, cause symptoms which are usually more horrific in appearance than real, but the problem should be avoided if possible. Leaves exhibiting shrivelled, fan-like distortions with multi-toothed margins are typical signs of damage from one of this family of weedkillers. The effects are usually not permanent, fresh leaves appearing after the fumes have dispersed, reverting to their normal shape, but damage at critical times of the year could prove serious in upsetting the vine's flowering.

This leaves us with three herbicide types which used in combination should answer all our problems. Paraquat/diquat herbicides such as Gramaxone, available to the gardener as Weedol will affect any green plant growth it touches, but will not be harmful if it touches bark. It acts in the presence of light, working fastest on sunny days. It is not residual and is quickly broken down by soil organisms, but is highly toxic if taken into the mouth. It kills annuals, but only burns off the tops of perennials which regrow later. Persistent use of this compound alone would eventually encourage perennials by means of eliminating annual competition. Perennials can be eliminated by using glyphosate herbicide, available as Tumbleweed. This is expensive but very effective if applied to weeds with a good leaf area in active growth. Like paraquat it is not residual, but unlike paraquat it is non-toxic to humans and animals.

In order to prevent the emergence of fresh weed seedlings we may apply Simazine to the soil surface. This forms an invisible barrier, as long as the soil is not afterwards cultivated, which kills young seedlings and keeps the soil free of weeds for up to six months. Ideally it should be applied in March or April to moist soil which is largely free of standing weeds. If there is only light weed cover it may be applied in combination with Weedol in the same spray, but if weed growth is already heavy it is better to burn this off with Weedol alone a fortnight before applying the Simazine. Simazine is residual and should not be used near vines less than two years old, nor anywhere for more than two or three years running without a break.

Never use mist sprayers for herbicide application. Use either a fine rose or dribble-bar on a watering can or a "Polijet" low pressure fan nozzle on a knapsack sprayer. If the paraquat/ Simazine combination is applied in the spring, the perennials will have made enough regrowth for the effective application of glyphosphate in June or July. Once rid of weeds it is a simple matter to prevent their re-establishment by spot treatment of the appropriate herbicide as required. It is a classical case of the "stitch in time". The more weeds become established the harder they are to clear.

CHAPTER 7

Propagation

The only way to propagate a vine variety is by some form of cutting. Seeds never come true and seedlings as explained before almost always produce poorer vines than their parents. There are all sorts of weird and wonderful methods of propagation recommended but only one is worth spending any time on, and that is the "long cutting" method. Two requirements are necessary, firstly light soil and secondly good cutting material. Do not be tempted to propagate from wood of some unknown variety just because it has been given to you. There is a great likelihood of it being some utterly unsuitable variety.

Cuttings should be of two or three buds and nine to twelve inches in length. The wood must be healthy, ripe and sturdy. Black lumps on the outside of the wood indicate the winter spore clusters of botrytis mildew and such wood should be destroyed. The cutting should be trimmed so that the bottom cut is made just below a bud. This trimming to size is best done at winter pruning time in January or February but they should be stored under moist but light soil until late March to protect them from drying out and the frost. In March they are set the right way up in light soil so that the top bud is about two inches above the surface, and they should be heeled in firmly. The cuttings remain in this position for a year. Provided they are of good quality, the soil is light and you avoid mildews and nematodes a good percentage should strike roots and put out shoots. They may be lifted in the following spring and planted in their final position. It must be remembered of course that whereas a rooted vine will bear fruit only two and a half years after planting, starting from a cutting will take a year longer.

Grafting is really beyond all but the most dedicated amateurs as it requires great skill and special equipment such as heated propagating boxes. For reasons already mentioned grafting offers no advantages in Britain.

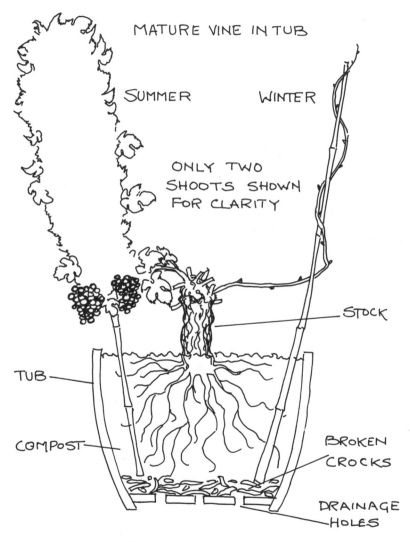

MATURE VINE IN TUB

SUMMER   WINTER

ONLY TWO
SHOOTS SHOWN
FOR CLARITY

STOCK

TUB

COMPOST

BROKEN
CROCKS

DRAINAGE
HOLES

Fig. 11.   Mature vine in tub.

CHAPTER 8

Vines in Pots or Tubs

Those of us fortunate enough to have gardens tend to forget that many either have no garden at all or possibly only one the size of a pocket handkerchief. Others have the space but only in the shape of a slab of concrete. The colossal sale of growbags in recent years has emphasised this point, and has enabled us to turn barren corners into verdant mini-jungles. I would not recommend any perennial be grown in a growbag, but patios and courtyards are brightened up with pots and tubs, and these can be used for grapevines.

Naturally one cannot grow a vine to its normal size unless the container is very large, but if the plant is kept to a size proportional to the volume of its holder there is no reason why you should not produce some prime grapes. There is of course no upper limit to the size of the container, and I would not like to be specific regarding the lower limit, but for practical purposes it is probably not worth while using anything less than a 12 inch pot. Even then you should not expect to get more than a couple of bunches a year. At the other end of the scale a hogshead barrel cut in half will provide homes for two quite sizeable plants yielding sensible crops.

All containers should be thoroughly cleaned before filling. Drainage holes should be provided if not already present. Tubs should have 2.5 cm (1 in) holes bored at intervals of about 20 cm (8 in) in the base, and the whole container should then be treated well with a wood preservative. Some brands are unsuitable for use in close proximity to plants, but Cuprinol supply a suitable grade in their range.

Before filling the container make sure that it is either in its final position or can easily be moved on wheels or castors when full, or you may find yourself with an immovable tub a long way from its proposed site. Place a layer of broken crocks over the drain holes to prevent water clogging and then top up with the growing medium. The nature of this material is critical. The vine's health will largely be governed by the amount of water and nutrients present. Both must be available in sufficiency, but not in excess.

This is really the nub of the matter and the smaller the volume of soil, the more difficult it is to maintain the balance of the conditions in it. If too much fertiliser is applied to a garden bed it is usually fairly soon absorbed by the great mass of soil and leached out, but in a confined container it can remain at a toxic level for an extended period and cause serious damage to the occupying plant. Similarly the moisture content is liable to rapid and wide variation unless the compost is of right consistency. Remember that your vine is going to have to live out its life in the same cramped home and if the soil is sick it cannot escape by reaching out for a healthier foothold. It is worth the trouble of making up a compost that drains freely while retaining a satisfactory water content and nutrient level. A mixture of one part sharp sand, two parts peat and four parts good loam should provide the desired characteristics.

At the outset you may wish to mix in some fertiliser such as John Innes base fertiliser at 3 or 4 oz/bushel, but if in doubt cut this rate down and supplement with a fortnightly liquid feed. Liquid feed will become necessary anyway because any added fertiliser will eventually become exhausted. Don't overdo feeding. It is easier to boost a weak vine than save one being poisoned by a toxic nutrient level.

During the first year of the vine's life only one shoot should be grown, all others being pinched out. If this shoot proves to be weak cut it back at the end of the year and repeat the performance in the following season. If on the other hand it is strong and the thickness of a pencil at a height of 30 cm (12 in) cut it back to that height during the winter. This growth will become the permanent stock. Two shoots may be allowed in the second year and they may fruit though it is more usual to take the first crop in the third summer. In the second winter cut back again leaving as many buds as you think the vine is capable of bearing shoots in the following season. (Fruiting shoots always spring from the past summer's growth.)

Each subsequent winter carry out the same treatment leaving more or less buds according to the vigour of the vine. A vine in a 12 in pot should be allowed to produce only one or two fruiting shoots each year, but a plant in a large tub may bear as many as a dozen shoots or more. Only experience with your particular container, vine variety and compost will tell you just how large your vine may be allowed to develop. To start with err on the mean side. Allow fewer shoots rather than more. After all it is better to have four plump, ripe bunches, than a dozen undersized clusters of sour green "peas". Sometimes it may be helpful to pinch out some flowers if the blooms are very numerous in order to ensure a high leaf-area-to-fruit-weight ratio.

Training is largely a matter of choice. Some sort of support for the growing shoots must be provided, but the form of support can be arranged to suit the surroundings. A plant in a 12 in pot will probably be happy with a single five foot cane up which to train the two shoots each summer, while a vine in a tub will require several canes arranged around the circumference of the tub in goblet form. Alternatively the vine may first be trained in standard form with a very high stock of over 90 cm (3 ft) instead of the normal 30 cm. The shoots springing from the head of the stock can then be allowed to hang freely unless in a windy position. Whatever training method is used the growing shoots should be stopped at about 120 cm (4 ft). If the shoots do not make four feet it is probably a sign that you have tried to grow too many, but if four feet is easily achieved and vigorous regrowth follows stopping, you should allow more shoots in the following season.

Apart from the attractiveness of vines grown in this way some excellent if limited quantities of fruit may be cropped, but never forget that the performance of any plant in a container will depend on the attention you pay to its condition.

CHAPTER 9

Vines Under Glass

The object of a greenhouse or conservatory is to provide an artificially warm climate so that plants otherwise unsuited to cope with our latitudes can be made to thrive and bear crops. In practice this widens considerably the number of grapevines we can grow, and pushes further north the limits of vine culture. Indeed a greenhouse situated in the most northerly extremes of Britain will ripen many varieties without the need to resort to artificial heat. The factor which decides whether a variety is for outdoor or glasshouse culture is the local climate. There is no point whatsoever in growing a vine under glass if it will produce good fruit outside. It is merely a waste of house space. On the other hand it is pointless trying to crop a vine outdoors if it is only suited to house culture in your area. It will grow perfectly happily, but it will not ripen its grapes. Mueller-Thurgau will ripen very well every season outdoors in southern counties, will benefit from a wall north of the Wash and will often need the protection of glass north of Yorkshire. From this it will be seen that one cannot be specific when classifying grapes according to their form of culture. Of course there are many vines which will only do well under glass even in the south, though they may be perfectly happy in the open in Spain or Italy. Some varieties are so demanding as to require a little supplied heat, particularly early in the season, but the cost of heating is now so exorbitant as to make the culture of such exotics an expensive luxury. This is especially true when there are so many vines which will give excellent results in an unheated house, so I shall confine myself to these here.

One normally associates the glasshouse with dessert grapes, but there is no reason why those living in the colder parts of the country should not grow grapes for wine inside. A list of predominantly wine-producing varieties has been given in Chapter 3. It is true that the very best quality dessert fruit require glass in our climate, though not for climatic reasons alone. The appearance of first class dessert fruit is important and a greenhouse eliminates any chance of imperfections due to weather damage.

The following is far from comprehensive, but gives a range of varieties suitable for the greenhouse.

GREENHOUSE VARIETIES – WHITE

Golden Chasselas. A very popular, fine flavoured grape with golden, translucent berries. One of the earliest, ripening outdoors in warm summers in good sites.

Mireille. Early, muscat flavoured, large berries.

Buckland Sweetwater. Early, prolific, well flavoured variety with heavy bunches of pale amber grapes.

Foster's Seedling. A free setting, early, very juicy grape of good flavour.

Lady Hutt. A vigorous mid-season grape. Flavour excellent.

Mrs Pearson. Similar characteristics to Lady Hutt, but ripening a little later.

Muscat of Alexandria. Very fine flavour, but requiring hand pollination with varieties such as Black Hamburg or Foster's Seedling. Also only recommended for culture in the south without additional heat.

GREENHOUSE VARIETIES – BLACK

Black Hamburg. The most popular black coldhouse vine in the country with very large black berries. It sets fruit very well and is highly recommended – though *not* for outdoors as is still sometimes advocated. The famous Hampton Court vine is of this variety.

Muscat Hamburg. A quality muscat grape which ripens comparatively early. It benefits from the presence of another pollinator variety.

Mrs Prince. A vigorous, mid-season, fine grape requiring hand pollination.

Muscat Champion. A mid-season, red berried grape which sets quality grapes freely.

Alicante. A late season vigorous variety requiring hard pruning.

TYPES OF HOUSE

Greenhouses fall into three main categories. The warmest is a south-facing lean-to backing on to a wall. The wall acts as a heat store, trapping solar energy during the day and releasing it at night. This greatly reduces the temperature variation and makes it possible to grow particularly fussy varieties which need extra warmth. Free-standing, span glasshouses (Fig. 12) are the type most commonly seen. They retain less heat at night, but are perfectly adequate for many varieties. Indeed the even less heat-retentive polythene tunnel will be perfectly suitable for most of the house vines normally found in Britain.

The main restriction on house suitability is that of size. Some grapes are very vigorous, and these should only be grown in the medium to large size garden greenhouse. Others can be reasonably restricted and grown in the smallest houses. Remember that the greenhouse climate encourages more vigorous growth than that normally experienced outside. The size of the vine must be firmly controlled by hard pruning. This need for space is increased by the necessity of having ample room between the supporting wires and the glass or polythene. Foliage in contact with the house can be scorched by the sun or mildewed due to condensation trapped between leaf and glass. With frequent and careful attention the wires can be as close 30 cm (12 in) to the glass, but failure to tie in and pinch out growth constantly will lead to trouble at this spacing, and a gap of 45 cm (18 in) is much safer. Methods of fixing the wires will depend on the construction of the house, but only galvanised wire of at least 2.5 mm diameter should be used, and it must be firmly secured under reasonable tension. When you set it up try to picture the weight of a mature vine bearing a heavy crop. After all, that is your aim!

PLANTING

Vines may be planted either inside or outside the house. Traditionally the plant is rooted outside and then led through a hole in the footing wall into the house. The object is to leave the floor of the house available for other crops and make the vine find its nutrients and water elsewhere. Alternatively the vine may be planted in the border of the house itself. Vines rooted outside the house may be planted in same way as normal outdoor varieties, but rather more preparation must be done to a house border before planting inside. It is not easy maintaining a good soil structure under cover because normal weathering is prevented and moisture must be added by artificial means, often employing hard water from the mains. The growing medium should be such that it retains nutrients and water without becoming waterlogged. This requires

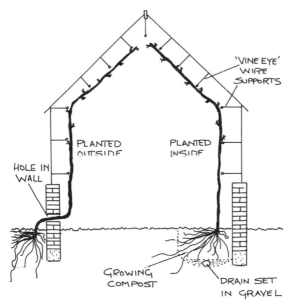

Fig. 12. Greenhouse layout showing vines trained to vertical arms.

either the presence of a naturally free-draining soil underneath or artificial drains.

A good base for the border may be mixed from three parts loam, one part coarse sand and one part peat. Manure may be liberally forked in, but it must be well rotted. Its function is more one of soil conditioner than supplier of nutrients. Too much fertiliser will only encourage sappy growth at the expense of fruit potential. Tales of horses buried under vines are rife but that requirement is quite fallacious! The fertiliser needs of the greenhouse vine is much the same as those described for outdoor plants in Chapter 4, but allowances should be made for the size of the vine and its root spread.

The spacing of vines depends very much on how large you intend each plant to grow. You may have one vine eventually taking up an entire house or you may decide on the greater interest of several smaller vines of various varieties. Within the limits of the vine's natural vigour, the house microclimate will allow you to prune your plants to the size you require.

TRAINING

During the first year the plant is treated exactly as if it were an outdoor vine. Only one strong bud is allowed to develop into a shoot and all laterals are pinched out to assist the leader. It is normal practice to train house-vines on the spur pruning principle. The permanent arms carrying the spurs may be horizontal or vertical (Fig. 13). If you intend to train horizontal arms the method is precisely the same as that employed for outdoor high-vigour vines already described. The alternative vertical arm is extended to its full length in the same manner, but is led straight to the peak of the house. Wood selected during winter pruning for arm extension should be at least the thickness of a pencil. Never be tempted to tie in weak canes. In the long run they will only increase the time required to grow the vine to its desired size and shape.

The formation period of the vine arm, or arms, will vary depending on the fertility of the soil and the natural vigour of the vine variety. A vine with two short horizontal arms or one vertical arm may be fully shaped in two seasons, or it may take three or even four seasons to reach its ultimate form. Bearing in mind that fruiting shoots spring from the previous year's wood, it is possible that grapes could be formed as early as the second year. This is really too early because they will absorb energy which should be spent in extending the vine, and the bunches should be pinched out before flowering. From the third summer on fruit may be cropped though this should be limited to a few bunches until the vine reaches its ultimate size.

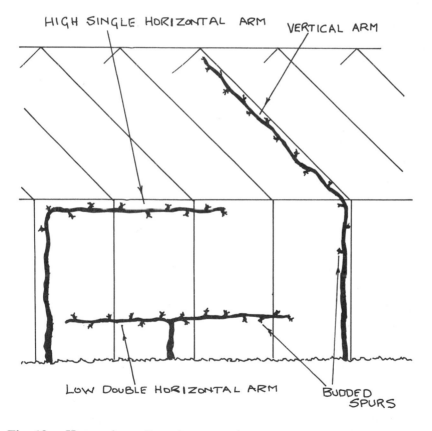

Fig. 13.   House vines after winter pruning to spurs on permanent arms.

THE GROWING SEASON

Though outdoor vines do not normally break bud until late April, those under glass may begin growth as much as two months earlier. Frosts are still a danger at this time of the year and care must be taken to close the house at night. Before the vines break dormancy those trained in the vertical arm form should be untied from their wire and laid upon the floor of the huse. If left upright the sap pressure will be greatest at the highest spurs resulting in uneven growth up the arm. As soon as the young shoots have emerged the arm may be retied to its wire. Care must be taken with this operation because the emerging shoots are very tender and can easily be snapped off. Horizontal arm trained vines may be left in their permanent position because their spurs being at the same level will be subject to a more even sap pressure.

Just as growth may precede that of outdoor vines by up to two months, so may flowering. Successful flowering depends on satisfactory pollination and fertilisation which are encouraged by warmth and adequate, (but not excessive), humidity. Damping down the house floor and careful attention to house ventilation should provide the ideal conditions. Many varieties, like most outdoor vines, are self-fertile, but some require pollinators. But self-fertile or not, the natural pollinating agent, wind, is seldom present in a house, and a little help with a soft brush or rabbit's tail in the same manner employed with peaches will ensure good fruitset. Once the berries have formed it is advisable to reduce the humidity in the house and increase the ventilation as much as possible on warm days, closing the house only at night or if the days are chilly.

Some varieties produce nice open clusters while others give a tighter bunch, but in either case if we wish to grow the largest, most attractive grapes we must reduce the number of berries in each cluster. When winegrowing the size of each individual berry is of no importance. The quality and quantity of juice is all that matters, and fifty small berries are as good as twenty large ones. However dessert grapes are undoubtedly more enjoyable if they are large. One cannot be specific as to how much one should thin the fruitlets. Often it is better to thin twice, once just after fruitset, and again about three weeks later, using pointed scissors. Fruitlets are removed evenly throughout the bunch so that the remainder have room to expand. If fruitset has been poor for some reason or other, a certain amount of natural thinning may have occurred so it is worth waiting to see that all the berries are swelling before reducing their number with scissors.

As the fruit develops maintain a steady water supply by frequent, light watering so that there is adequate moisture for berry swelling. Infrequent heavy watering may result in the grapes splitting, and too little water will result in small fruit. When the grapes become attractive to wasps and birds the greenhouse has a tremendous advantage in that the doors and ventilators can be fitted with gauze screens to keep pests out. Screens should be just fine enough to prevent wasps entry, but not so fine as to obstruct ventilation more than is absolutely necessary.

MILDEWS

Vines under cover do not become saturated with rain or dew, but they receive far less ventilation than outdoor plants and mildew is therefore still a problem. House conditions most commonly favour Oidium which is frequently seen on badly tended vines. Spraying is essential, the programme recommended for outdoor vines being adequate, though great care should be taken to avoid scorch caused by spraying in full sunlight, or at too great a concentration. Fungicides should be applied in the evening, the plant tissue being thoroughly covered in a fine mist, but not drenched.

CHAPTER 10

Vinification

It is not the aim of this book to go too deeply into winemaking, which is really a very large and complex subject, but it is hardly fair to tell you how to grow good grapes and then give no advice on turning them into good wine. I am going to assume that the majority of readers will already have at least a little country winemaking experience and be familiar with the fundamentals and terminology. Those who have no previous experience at all should refer to the bibliography in the appendix.

When I first started producing grapes I found my previous country winemaking experience very useful, but it must be realised that there are certain differences between making country wines and, if you will forgive the phrase, "real" winemaking. Of all fruits the wine grape is the only one which has been bred for making wine so it is hardly surprising that this fruit is unsurpassable for this purpose. Dessert grapes will only make very ordinary wine because they lack some of the ingredients necessary for the production of fine wine, but even the best wine grapes can be made into the worst wine if the correct procedure is not followed.

Grapegrowing ends and winemaking begins, of course, with the harvest which as it has already been stated is usually in mid-October. It is important that no grapes are picked that cannot be processed the same day because the fruit, and with it the juice, will start to deteriorate soon after being picked. The weight of bunches pressing on each other will cause juice to be spilt and the wild yeasts on the grape bloom will start poor ferments. Also oxidation of the juice will take place, causing loss of delicacy and flavour. English wines, like some German wines, are delicate and flowery and at every stage in the winemaking process efforts must be made to preserve this special quality.

Yeast starter. Two or three days before picking is due to take place you should make up a good yeast starter according to the recommended culture instructions, but using grape juice which has been pasteurised by keeping at 85° for 30 minutes and then cooled. As you are trying to make the best quality wine it is foolish to use any but the best yeasts. Never use general purpose yeasts but try to find a yeast culture that will be appropriate to your wine. If you are making a white wine use a Mosel-type yeast and if you are making a red or rosé use a Burgundy type. It is worth going to the slight extra expense of using a liquid culture as they are generally 100% what they claim to be. Due to the difficulty of preparing pure dry cultures, they tend to be contaminated with other strains. The commercial vineyards in England use cultures supplied by continental wine institutes but unfortunately these are not available to the amateur.

Milling. The first step in processing grapes is to split their skins by crushing them. The aim of milling is to render grapes more capable of yielding their juice on pressing because grapes whose skins are intact will tend to cushion each other and will not burst easily. Unless you have a vast crop it is not necessary to have a proper grapemill as they may easily be crushed by hand or even trodden if you wish!

A grapemill is rather like a mangle whose rollers have been separated by about an eighth of an inch to prevent the stalks and pips being crushed, thereby releasing excessive tannin and other substances into the juice. All parts of the apparatus must be made of non-metallic or stainless materials to prevent metal contamination causing a casse to form in the wine later.

When all your grapes have been crushed, the next step in vinification will depend on whether you are making a red, white or rosé wine. Firstly we will look at the white fermentation and later consider the differences which apply to a red or rosé ferment.

Vinification of White Juice. As soon as the grapes have been milled they should be pressed. For small quantities of fruit it is not even necessary to have a press, and on several occasions in the past I have coped with grapes from the garden by simply wringing the juice out of the grapes held in a piece of terylene net. Needless to say, if your crop is substantial a small press is a great asset. The juice from the press should be collected in a vessel such as a carboy and at the first opportunity sulphur dioxide must be introduced into it to both prevent oxidation and sterilise it. The further north one travels the poorer is the quality of the yeast in the bloom of the grape, and in the northern Europe almost all wine is now made using specially selected yeast cultures. Sulphur dioxide is introduced into the juice most simply, by means of the addition of sodium metabisulphite.

Sodium metabisulphite should be dissolved in the juice at a rate of 0.8 grammes per gallon. A chemist will weigh this out for you if you have no balance, but it is a good idea to order some of this compound in advance in case he has none in stock. Alternatively Campden tablets may be used. These consist of potassium metabisulphite, one tablet containing the approximate equivalent of 0.5 grammes of sodium metabisulphite.

Do not heavily overdo sulphiting or you will not find it easy to start the ferment. The juice is now safe for a while from spoilage and it should be left to settle for 24–48 hours. During this period the grape pulp particles and dust which has passed through the press will fall to the bottom, leaving clear juice above it. However, before settling actually begins, the sugar content and the acidity of the juice must be measured and adjusted if necessary.

Juice sugar content. Most of the German table wines and many of those from the Loire, Chablis and even Burgundy are, before fermentation, chaptalised, i.e., they have a small amount of sugar added to the juice to ensure that the final alcohol content will be sufficient to enable the wine to keep well. English grape juice also often needs some degree of chaptalisation, but if you have grown your grapes properly it should amount to no more than two or three ounces per gallon. In good years it may prove unnecessary even this far north. A hydrometer will quickly give you the gravity of your juice but remember to correct the reading for temperature, especially as the juice is often very cold at this time of the year. The hydrometer will be calibrated for a specific temperature. For every 5°C below that temperature you should subtract 0.001 from the specific gravity reading. Conversely for every 5°C above the calibration temperature add 0.001. Approximately 0.002 should be deducted from the reading to allow for the effect of suspended pulp.

Table 4 shows the amount of sugar to add to each gallon of juice requiring correction. As viticulture in this country is so similar to that of Germany we have taken to using much of their technique and terminology. This applies amongst other things to the specific gravity scale and we use the degree Oechsle or °Oe. This is very simply arrived at by converting 1.075 to 75° and 1.103 to 103° and so on. If your grapes have failed to reach 55° you will produce rather poor wine, and if the gravity is less than 50° you might as well not bother with it. If the juice is that bad you are growing the wrong variety! Normally, however, your grapes should produce a gravity of around 60–70°, but it may be much higher.

The ideal gravity for juice that is to be made into English wine is about 82° after chaptalisation. This will yield a potential alcohol content of around 11%. Do not be tempted to chaptalise to a higher gravity as too high on alcohol content would be incompatible in an English wine and destroy its delicacy.

Juice Acidity. Most varieties grown in suitable areas will not produce excessively acid juice in the average year, and indeed the acidity must be at a reasonable level or the wine will be dull and lifeless. Nevertheless it is necessary to measure the acidity of grape juice and make adjustments if required. The acidity is not likely to be too low in this country, but it may be a little high when late varieties have experienced cool summers.

Table 4 – Adjustment of juice sugar content

Natural juice gravity	°Oe	Potential alcohol % by vol.	Amount of sugar to add to bring gravity to 82°Oe	
			to 4.5 litres	to one gallon
1.050	50	6.5	365 g	13 oz
1.055	55	7.2	310 g	11 oz
1.060	60	7.8	252 g	9 oz
1.065	65	8.6	200 g	7 oz
1.070	70	9.2	140 g	5 oz
1.075	75	9.9	85 g	3 oz
1.080	80	10.6	28 g	1 oz
1.082	82	11.0	–	–

Plate 29.   Using the refractometer to measure sugar content.

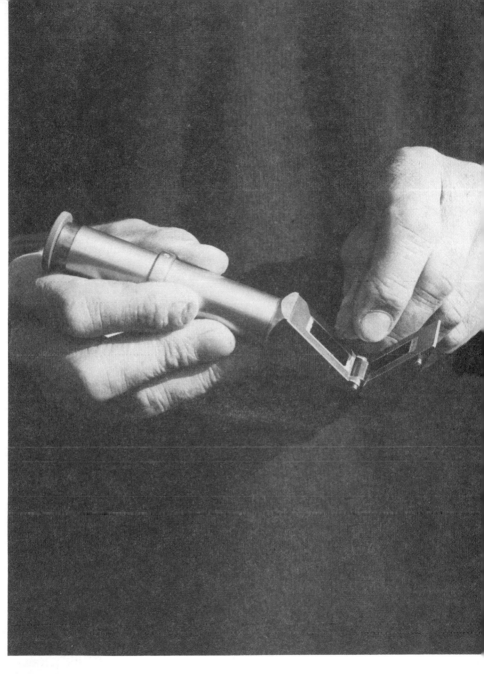

Plate 30. Squeezing a drop of grape juice on to refractometer prism.

Although I have assumed that you can read a hydrometer to measure the sugar content, not every winemaker is familiar with the technique of titration, the method by which we measure acidity. There is nothing difficult about it, as a simple description will demonstrate. The necessary apparatus and material suppliers are listed in the appendix.

Apparatus required:

1 5 ml pipette
1 25 ml graduated burette
   and stand
1 250 ml conical flask

Chemicals required:

N/10 (decinormal) Sodium
   Hydroxide
Distilled water
1% Phenolphthalein

Method

First rinse the 5 ml pipette with some of the juice, then draw juice up into the pipette past the graduation mark by sucking. Try to avoid the temptation of guzzling juice and remember it is potential wine! Quickly place your fingertip over the top end to prevent the juice running straight out and then by easing the finger up let the juice slowly drop out until the bottom of the surface meniscus is level with the graduation mark. You now have exactly 5 ml juice in the pipette and this is allowed to run into the conical flask which has previously been rinsed with distilled water. Be careful not to splash the sides and when the pipette has finished dripping, lightly touch the surface of the juice with the tip of the pipette to draw off the last drop. (Do not blow it out). Next add two drops only of 1% phenolphthalein solution. (If you are dealing with a coloured juice, previously decolourise a quantity by shaking it with a teaspoonful of activated charcoal.)

The graduated burette is then filled with decinormal sodium hydroxide solution. Take care with this liquid; it is caustic. If you have filled the burette above the zero mark open the tap and run some out into a container until the level is at or below the zero mark. Next note the level in the burette and place the conical flask beneath the tap. A little at a time the sodium hydroxide is run into the flask which is frequently but gently shaken to mix the contents. As soon as the contents take on a pink colour which fails to disappear on shaking, you have reached the neutral point and the

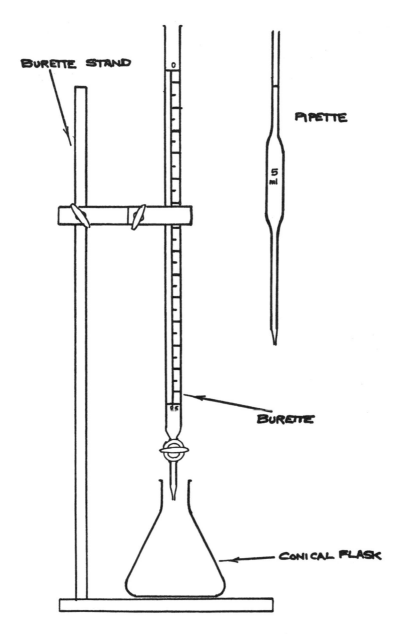

Fig. 14.   Acid determination apparatus.

level in the burette should be noted again. By subtracting the first reading from the second you can deduce the volume of sodium hydroxide that was required to neutralise the juice acid. Repeat the measurement two or three times to make sure that you are getting consistent results then divide the average result by 10. The figure you arrive at is the acidity of the grape juice expressed as % sulphuric acid. If this figure is below 0.65% the acidity of your juice needs no correction, but if it is higher it must be reduced.

The acids in your juice will be mainly tartaric and malic acids. Acid reduction by means of chalk is perfectly satisfactory as long as it is not overdosed. The first acid to be neutralised by chalk will be the tartaric acid and one may remove all this acid without ill effect, but if any of the malic acid is reduced in this way calcium salts are formed which affect the taste adversely. When grapes are ripe most of the acid in the juice is tartaric, but the less ripe the grapes the higher will be the proportion of malic acid. It is probably safe to assume that at least 25% of the juice acidity will be due to tartaric, and as all of this can safely be removed with chalk, if the acidity is less than 0.88% an addition of precipitated chalk will solve the problem. 3.0 grammes of chalk will reduce the acidity of 4.5 litres (1 gallon) of juice by 0.1%.

If the juice acidity is higher than 0.88% the safest way to reduce the acidity is by dilution with water. If your grapes are consistently over acid, grow an earlier variety.

The Fermentation. After your juice has been adjusted for sugar and acid if necessary and settled for 24–48 hours, it should be racked off the pulp sediment into another carboy which should be an ambient temperature of about 18°–21°C. The juice is now ready for inoculation with the yeast starter, and after it has been added a fermentation lock is placed in the neck of the vessel.

Do not expect the juice to burst into life immediately. There may still be a fairly high level of sulphur dioxide in it which, although it will not kill the yeast, may retard it for a while. Gradually the sulphur dioxide will be neutralised and when it falls below a certain level the fermentation will start. Do not worry about the waiting period; after all, if the yeast will not work, nothing else will, since bacteria and wild yeasts are far more vulnerable to sulphur dioxide. If the fermentation has not started after a week it probably means that you overdosed the metabisulphite and an aerating racking should remedy the situation.

Once the ferment starts the temperature of the space in which the fermentation vessel is placed should be reduced to around 13–16°C. If the fermentation takes place in too warm a place it will be very violent and it will work itself out too quickly. This must be avoided or much of the bouquet and character of the wine will be lost. If the ferment is allowed to overheat, it may even reach a temperature at which the yeast will be killed. Remember that grape juice has all the necessary requirements for the yeast and you will not need to add nutrients. The main task is to control the speed of the ferment rather than boost it. The ideal fermentation period is about three weeks and unless the temperature is very low it will seldom take much longer.

Racking. When the fermentation has ceased the wine is allowed to stand for up to six weeks and then it should be carefully racked off the dead yeast into a clean carboy.

Never allow the wine to stay on the old yeast for longer than six weeks or you will run the risk of yeast casse, easily recognised as a disgusting "mousey" flavour and aftertaste in the wine. This is caused by the enzymes in the yeast digesting the yeast cells themselves and the results are disastrous. Carry out racking with as little disturbance and splashing as possible and add further sodium metabisulphite at the rate of 0.4 grammes per 4.5 litres (gallon). The vessel should be topped up, leaving as little air space as possible, and if the vessel is too large the contents should be broken down into smaller containers. The containers should now be placed in the coolest room available.

The wine will have sufficient alcohol in it to depress the freezing point by three or four degrees and as long as the temperature of the wine does not fall below −4°C it will not freeze. Lowering the temperature of the wine will help to stabilise it, especially as far as tartrates are concerned. The appearance of crystals on the bottom of the wine vessel indicates that unstable tartaric acid is being precipitated out as the insoluble potassium bitartrate and calcium tartrate salts. This is desirable since it prevents the same thing happening later in the bottle. If crystals *do* appear in the bottle it will not affect the taste, but you do not want to get a spoonful of gritty crystals in your glass.

Red and Rosé Fermentation. We have now dealt with the process of white vinification but there are certain differences for red and rosé ferments which should be appreciated. As the colour of these wines is derived from the skin of the grape it is obvious that the skins must remain in contact with the juice long enough to allow the desired degree of colour extraction to take place. This means that the ferment is started on the whole pulp and not just the juice as with white wine. As grape stalks contain a high level of tannin, the best red wines are made from pulps from which the stalks have previously been removed. Destalking is usually done even before the grapes have passed through the mill.

After milling the pulp and juice are collected in a container such as a polythene dustbin where the first stages of the ferment can take place. You should make certain that the dustbin is made either of polythene or polypropylene and *not* polyvinyl chloride (PVC) which usually contains toxic plasticisers which can poison the wine – and you! Sulphur dioxide is added to the pulp at the same rate as recommended for white juice. This ensures safety from wild ferments and oxidation. The next step is to take a sample of juice and determine and adjust if necessary the sugar and acid level as detailed above in the description of the white vinification. However when determining the acid level of red juice it is necessary to remove the natural colour of the juice to avoid confusion. A small teaspoon of activated charcoal shaken with enough juice for the test will decolourise it quickly and the charcoal is removed simply by filtering or decanting.

The bin should be placed in a reasonably warm place (about 17–21°C), then the yeast starter is added and the lid put in place. As with the white juice the ferment may not start immediately but it will before long and the bin should then be moved to a cooler place, (about 15°C), to prevent the ferment becoming too violent. The fermenting pulp should be turned twice a day until the desired juice colour has been achieved, which may take between one and seven days, but is usually about three days. The alcohol produced in the early stages of fermentation will aid extraction of the colour, but it is wise to have your wine paler rather than darker than your ideal.

100

This is because tannin is extracted with the colour and excess tannin causes harshness. Those who wish to go more deeply into the subject will learn that excess tannin can be fined out with gelatine. As soon as you are satisfied with the colour you should put your fermenting pulp through the press and continue the fermentation in a vessel such as a carboy under a lock. The remainder of the process is as for white wine.

Fining. More detailed coverage of fining and the simple tests you can carry out to see if it is required will be found in other books (see appendix), but it is worth saying a few words here. Fining carried out properly takes nothing from a wine but an imbalance, but if carried out clumsily or overdone it can strip much of the quality and character from the wine.

When wine is freshly made it usually contains one or two unstable compounds so that although the wine may look crystal clear at the time of bottling there is no guarantee that it will remain so. Commercially speaking fining is standard procedure to ensure that the bottle of wine that you buy is in a condition in which it will not spoil on keeping. Certain substances in the wine can under various conditions cause unsightly hazes. Imagine, for example, a wine made from grapes grown in a poor summer. The chances are that it will contain excessive protein which may not be at all apparent to the eye when the wine is bottled in the cool of March. Unless the wine is stored in a very cool cellar it will warm up a little in the summer and as it warms up a haze due to the excess protein may form in the wine. It will probably taste no different but it does not look very nice! This type of haze is a colloid, and no amount of filtering will remove it. In fact it consists of millions of minute particles all of which carry the same electrostatic charge. In the case of our example the charge will be positive. As you will know, like charges repel each other and so the particles can not settle out and lie together on the bottom. The only way to cure this haze is by a calculated addition of a substance carrying the opposite charge. In this case a measured quantity of Bentonite, which is negatively charged, is stirred into the wine so that the unlike charges may neutralise each other and allow the haze particles to settle out.

Sweetening. Usually, unless you have been clever enough to grow especially late botrytis-infected grapes, your wine will ferment out absolutely dry. This may not be to your taste, but there is nothing to prevent your sweetening with sugar to suit your palate. Commercially nearly all German table wines are sweetened after fermentation because the market palate has come to like them that way. Commercial wine may only be sweetened by using some of the original grape sugar, but there is no reason why we as amateurs should not use ordinary cane or beet white sugar. A typical sweetening rate is about 50 grammes of sucrose or white sugar to 4.5 litres (gallon) of wine, but you will have to experiment to see if that suits you.

One thing you must remember, however, if you sweeten your wine, is that it will be liable to fermentation if certain precautions are not taken. You cannot rely on sulphur dioxide preventing fermentation as a good wine yeast will be unaffected by any level of sulphiting which cannot be tasted. The only way to bottle sweet table wine with no danger of fermentation taking place later, is to pass the wine through a filter to remove any stray yeast cells. To the ill informed who object to filtering I would point out that it is standard practice with commercial wines. The purpose of filtering is not to clear the wine, but to remove the occasional yeast cell or any odd particle such as bentonite or that picked up from a barrel which might appear as an unsightly "floater" in your glass.

Happily suitable filters are now available to the amateur (see appendix).

Bottling. This operation usually takes place in the March or April following the harvest. I consider aesthetics important in wine and it is worth trying to find a suitable type of bottle for your produce. If you are growing white wine it is a good idea to use a Hock or Mosel bottle; for a red or rosé the same bottle is equally suitable (many German reds have no special bottle of their own). We have no traditional bottle of our own in England and as our wines most closely resemble those of Germany it seems appropriate that we should use their bottles. This is of course a matter of personal choice and if you prefer the Burgundy bottle by all means use it.

Make sure that the bottles are spotless and then rinse them with a solution made up by dissolving 10 grammes of sodium metabisulphite in a pint of water, and leave them to drain for a few minutes before filling. Use the best possible corks which should be soaked for 24 hours in cold water first and then rinsed in the same sodium metabisulphite solution. Lead capsules always look best but they require a rather expensive capsuling machine, and capsules of the viscap type are adequate for the amateur and pleasing to the eye.

Maturing. I remember some years ago believing the old fallacy that the older a wine, the better it is. Normally English wine, like German table wine, is at its best between one and four years old. Few people will have the will power to leave a bottle more than four years, but even if you have, do not do so. Usually northern wines do not keep for very long and after about four years they will slowly decline in quality. On the other hand do not drink it too quickly and try to put off opening your first bottle until the Christmas after bottling. A little bottle maturity will improve the wine noticeably.

If your wine shows signs of darkening in colour it is a sure sign that oxidation has set in due to the fact that you were a bit mean with the metabisulphite or that you did not keep the wine topped up before bottling. Oxidation is disastrous as it completely destroys the charm and character of the wine, quickly converting it to an insipid watery "sherry". Try to store your wine in a cool place, but more particularly in a place where the temperature does not fluctuate rapidly.

When to drink your Wine. Almost any time is suitable for drinking English wine as it accompanies many dishes perfectly, but remember that it is delicate and flowery so do not drown it with strong flavours. Chill white wines but do not over-chill them or so much will be missed by the palate. Good English wines are unsurpassed in their bouquet so take your time and enjoy them. On a winter's evening in front of the fire you can enjoy again the fragrance of a summer's day, but perhaps one of the loveliest ways of appreciating your wine is to drink it unaccompanied by food while sitting in the garden on just such a sunny summer's day.

If you have grown your grapes properly and made your wine with care you will know the satisfaction of drinking a wine which would be priced at well over a pound a bottle in a wineshop, and into the bargain it will have cost you less than the cheapest country wine. What more can one ask of life?

POMACE WINE

It is possible to make a delightful country wine from the grape pomace which comes from the press. You may have a reasonable quantity of pomace from your own grapes or you may be able to purchase some at small cost from a local vineyard. You will not normally obtain it free as vineyards spread it as a high grade fertiliser.

The procedure for pomace wine is simple but great care must be taken to prevent oxidation which will ruin the freshness of this light wine. Firstly it is vitally important that the pomace is fresh from the press and has not been lying around for more than a few minutes. It should immediately be placed in a covered bin and sulphited at about 20 grammes of sodium metabisulphite per dustbinful.

Let us say that the pomace you have originally yielded 90 litres (20 gallons) of grape juice. You should add half that quantity, 45 litres (10 gallons), of water to the pomace and allow it to soak for two days well covered. Stirring should be minimised to prevent oxidation. Prodding is a better way of agitating it. After two days the pomace is pressed again and the liquid is collected in a fermenting vessel. During the soak it will have taken up a lot of flavour from the grape pomace and also a little sugar. Measure the gravity of the liquid which will be somewhere in the region of 10°Oe. You should now chaptalise this up to about 70°Oe so that the resulting country wine will contain about 9% alcohol. The following table will give you the additions of cane sugar to add.

Chaptalisation of pomace wine

Initial gravity (°Oe)	Amount of sugar to add:	
	to each 4.5 litre	to each gallon
5	784 g	1 lb 12 oz
10	756 g	1 lb 11 oz
15	700 g	1 lb 9 oz
20	616 g	1 lb 6 oz
25	560 g	1 lb 4 oz

After chaptalisation the procedure is precisely the same as for real wine as described earlier. The finished product should be grapey and fresh. It is light but still possesses a good flavour. It is ready to drink very young – almost as soon as it is clear, and should be finished within one year. It is a drink to enjoy when you feel you cannot justify opening one of your bottles of best wine. It has one great advantage in being light as it contains very few hangover-producing components and can be drunk greedily without ill effects!

Appendix

SUPPLIERS

Vines – Outdoor and Greenhouse
Cranmore Vineyard, Yarmouth, Isle of Wight. PO41 OXY

Secateurs – "Felco"
Your local garden shop or contact Burton, McCall and Co, 55 Welford Rd, Leicester. LE2 7AE for your nearest stockist.

Fungicides – see text
Your local garden shop or contact Murphy Chemical Ltd, Wheathampstead, St Albans, Herts. AL4 8QU Tel: 058-283-2001.

Grape Mills and Presses
Walker Desmond and Sons Ltd, Lever St, Hazel Grove, Stockport. SK7 4EN Tel: 061-483-3241.
Winemaker's Vineyard, 96 Brigstock Rd, Thornton Heath, Surrey. CR4 7JA.

Corking machines, Corks, Capsules
J. Perkins and Sons Ltd, Algarve House, 1 St Joan St, Blackfriars, London SE1 8DA.

Miscellaneous Winemaking Equipment
Southern Vinyards, Nizells Avenue, Hove, East Sussex.
Leigh Williams and Sons, Tattenhall, Nr Chester, CH3 9PT.
Vina Ltd, 49 Marsh Lane, Bootle, Liverpool. L20 4HY.

Bibliography

General Viticulture. A. J. Winkler. University of California Press.

Basic Viticulture. A. Massel. Heidelberg Publishers Ltd.

Basic Oenology. A. Massel. Heidelberg Publishers Ltd.

Der Weinbau. Prof. Vogt. Ulmer Stuttgart.

Viticulture Moderne. E. Chancrin and J. Long. Hachette.

Grapes under Glass. H. Parsons. Collingridge.

Scientific Winemaking Made Easy. J. R. Mitchell. Amateur Winemaker Publications.

First Steps in Winemaking. C. J. J. Berry. Amateur Winemaker Publications.

Wines from your Vines. N. Poulter. Amateur Winemaker Publications.

Conversion Table

Imperial to Metric

1 fluid ounce (fl oz)	= 28.4 millilitres (ml)
1 pint (pt)	= 568.3 millilitres (ml)
1 gallon (gal)	= 4.546 litres (l)
1 ounce (oz) (avoirdupois)	= 28.4 grammes (g)
1 pound (lb) (avoirdupois)	= 453.6 grammes (g)
1 inch (in)	= 2.54 centimetres (cm)

Metric to Imperial

1 litre (1000 millilitres)	− 1.76 pints
1 gramme	= 0.035 ounces
1 kilo (kg)	= 2.2 pounds
1 centimetre (cm)	= 0.3937 inches

Index